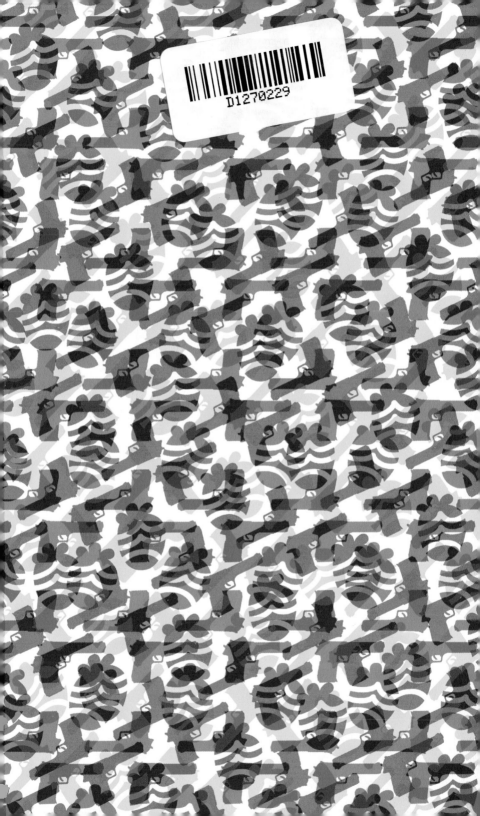

Babylon Street Elementary

Special Needs

I lost him. At Disneyland. At night. And all I could conjure up in my mind's crystal ball of worst-case scenarios were flashes of amusement-park carnage—toddlers flung out of teacups, old ladies stuffed under rollercoaster wheels, and me sobbing on the local news. When they asked me to describe him, I couldn't even remember what my nephew was wearing. I was in an amnesiac's panic: He has brown hair and brown eyes. He's shorter than me. He has a red cap on. I think it was red. I turned to my boyfriend, pleading: "What color was his cap? His cap. His cap! What color was it? Do you remember what Jojo was wearing? Tell the man. Tell the man what he was wearing." I demanded he help me remember, my frustration flaring up. Gregorio had this strange, twisting look on his face, a mix of annoyance and disappointment and pity. Pity that I could feel like hot bubbles in my stomach because I knew then that our time together, our five years of fighting and arguing, of trying to make us work, was now up. Our last chance was just there, between us, evaporating like the last, brackish puddle of a long-gone storm as we stood in the Lost Children Room off Main Street, U.S.A. I had given him what he needed to leave. And yet I couldn't attend to us. I needed to find Jojo. It was midnight and I was supposed to return him to my aunt in an hour. I lost both of them that night. I lost my nephew and my boyfriend right in front of Sleeping Beauty's Castle.

I called Gregorio my orange half. Not necessarily because he was my soul mate or better half, my media naranja as they say in Spanish, although I thought he was that, but because he was from Orange County and half the time he sounded much like an Orange-County conservative. He was actually born in Aguascalientes, Aguascalientes, but spent most of his life in Anaheim. So I always called him my orange half in honor of his adopted county. If one could be patriotic about a county, Gregorio was that. Even though we both lived in LA now, we spent every other weekend in the O.C. dining with Santa Ana relatives, attending lectures at UC Irvine or shopping at Fashion Island. Traffic en route to Anaheim often provided at least an hour of quality boyfriend time to argue over the merits of banda vs. salsa, gossip about uncles and aunts and their children's ghetto-chunty-dramas, or plan out our Southern Californian disposable-income to-do lists. I still had never visited Catalina Island or a Palm Springs nudist resort, nor had I ever even touched, much less stood by, a Joshua tree. Solvang. Mt. Baldy. The Four Seasons, Santa Barbara. My list for us grew every year.

Gregorio's own Californian Dreamin' was simple. His childhood fantasy was easy. He wanted to ride every ride at Disneyland. He dreamed of a day spent racing from Space Mountain to Peter Pan's Flight to the Jungle Cruise to Stars Tours—the works, all 50-some attractions in 24 hours. I hadn't been to Disneyland in a very long time. Perusing the amusement park's map after buying our tickets, I realized that there are way more rides available than when I was a kid, along with this entire new extra amusement park attached to the original. California Adventure is like one of those undeveloped parasitic twin heads with just hair and teeth attached to some poor Chinese girl whose family couldn't afford a removal operation. California Adventure wasn't OG enough for Gregorio, so we got to ignore the parasite. What we couldn't ignore were the masses and masses of people, tourists with villages of manic children in strollers and on leashes entering the park in unison. Parking was a bitch and Jojo got a little bit impatient as we waited in a snaking line to purchase our tickets.

Despite the obstacle of the crowds and the wait for our entrance, Gregorio, Jojo, and I had a prepared plan of action for the day. It is what you need at these places to get the most out of them. You need a system. It's what we needed if I was going to help Gregorio accomplish his dream.

But, understand, we weren't there simply because of Gregorio's childhood goal, but also as a way to work on our admittedly shaky relationship. The trip was an exercise our therapist had suggested.

It was during couple's therapy I pointed out to Ms. Shayla, our therapist, that Gregorio possessed the annoying, overachiever-wetback gene that completely opposed my slacker-pocho gene. I explained to her how often first-generation Latinos arrive in the U.S. barefoot, with fucked-up teeth and that big-ass booster-shot scar on their shoulders, but then go on to win the Nobel Peace Prize or start nine businesses while we Chicanos, who have been citizens for more than a hundred years, think getting an A.A. is an accomplishment. Gregorio was definitely of the former stock. With a couple of degrees and some small parcels of real estate, he had more education and capital than my entire family tree.

Gregorio is of the mind that all you have to do is work hard and squeeze the gold from the orbs of opportunity hanging up and down the freedom trees in America. He's verging on Republican but never checks that box on his voter registration card. I don't hold his politics against him because he's tenderhearted, kind, charitable, patient, and has a great job and a nice dick. He's the perfect candidate for husbandhood and fatherhood. Which is something he totally wants to be, a father—another reason we were in couple's therapy.

See, Gregorio wants to start his family. Like now. He wants the six-bedroom, luxury casa de adobe, the perritos, the rental properties, the 2.5 kids, along with the annual passes to the happiest place for traviesos on Earth. And I think I want that, too, but just not right now, right now. He's 37. I'm 32; the same age he was when we met. That's what this whole outing to Disneyland was supposed to be. It was the excursion Ms. Shayla recommended. It was a test. It was supposed to be fun, low-stakes practice for the family project we supposedly wanted to create together. She asked that we choose a goal that we could accomplish together in one day. Something fun and doable like on a reality show. She wanted us to work together to accomplish something and then evaluate the results at our next session. I was really trying to make it work, trying to align everything that Gregorio loves, trying to make him want me again in that initial I-just-met-you-last-week sort of way. He loves Disneyland, he wants to be a father, he loves me. The trip was supposed to bring all that together.

I grew up in Montebello, Los Angeles County. My family went to Disneyland all the time. The park was cool but nothing to obsess over, especially as an adult with a sliver of hetero-agoraphobia—fear of large spaces filled with herds of heterosexuals and their progeny. I got to go to Disneyland all the time when I was young. Gregorio, on the other hand, was like UNICEF poor when he arrived as a 10-year-old in the 1970s. The stories he shared with me about his pueblo poverty often made me feel sad, mad, and laugh all at the same time. The anecdotes jump-started my own internal nonprofit I called the Adopt-a-Chunty program. It's the internal love machine where you fall in love with a Mexican immigrant and try to fix everything in his life and make all his dreams come true as if he were dying of cancer. This heart impulse is irrespective of the fact Gregorio is today a systems analyst with a terrific, six-figure salary, working for a large corporation. He didn't need me for anything but companionship. To me, however, he was that adorable UNICEF boy with dimples and camel eyelashes and an easy dream.

He told me that it was only when he came to the U.S. that he realized, "Oh shit, I'm ... poor." Because in Aguascalientes, running around barefoot with teams of cousins and eating tortillas and salt everyday, it just seemed liked everyone in the world lived the same way. Shoes were for horses and mules, not children. But then came the dramatic month of his life when his family began to trek north in a series of carpools and bus rides. It was a journey that finally culminated in a long, long car ride from the border into what seemed like another dimension: Anaheim, California.

This long car ride included, of course, a quick passing-by of Disneyland. The car's driver sang to the drowsy occupants in the car, "Mira, mira las luces de Disneylandia!" They all awoke to gawk at the universe of electricity beaming from the park. The first time Gregorio glimpsed that small piece of the Alps called the Matterhorn and the sleek monorail and the billboards of animals that wore clothes with big buttons, he decided he liked the States United and, specifically, he wanted to go There. "What was in that place over There?" was the first question he asked of his new country. And finally, he received the opportunity, seven years later, in his senior year of high school, on Grad Night, but at that point he had to pretend that he liked girls and that he had been to Disneyland hundreds of times before, just like his classmates had, and that he didn't really like all the pussy rides at the park. All the boys complained about the lack of speed on the rides, and preferred to strategize about how to use the dark parts of the slow rides to press their erections up against their captive dates. Gregorio pretended to know what they were talking about. The dark parts? The thing was, he had a hard time not feeling his heart ache with wanting as he passed the pussy ride that had people levitating up and down inside flying elephants. He tried to not appear disappointed that some rides were not even considered by his high school clique and others were closed for renovation. Even I was surprised to learn he didn't know how to sing the chorus of that one song about how small the world is after all.

Of course, when I heard these confessions of a pobre, I took it as my duty to give my boyfriend the ultimate-drama-super-fucking-fragilistic Disneyland experience I could conjure.

Enter my nephew Jojo. He's actually my cousin. He's my older aunt's son, around my age, but because he has Down syndrome I've always treated him as if he were my younger nephew. We basically grew up together. He loves playing video games, making hot cocoa for guests, and sneaking up behind people to scare them. For a couple of months recently, he even worked at Jack-in-the-Box through some special-needs employees program until something happened that my aunt refuses to this day to divulge, and so the family just stopped asking about what happened at Jack-in-the-Box. But whenever she wants to reprimand Jojo, she gives him a real intense old chola stare and threatens, "Do you want me to take you back to Jack-in-the-Box?" Jojo gets real quiet. "OK then," she emphasizes with her drawn-in, arched eyebrows as my cousin gets real scared and falls in line. She is a good mother though. Don't get the wrong impression. She just discovered an easy way to control Jojo's moods—which, now that he's sort of a man weighing 200 pounds, can be real troublesome. Every year she treats Jojo to a trip to Disneyland. But she's no spring chola anymore. She's getting older and the trips take more out of her now. So I offered to take him in order to help her out and also because of what I discovered. Get this. I didn't know that if you have a special-needs child, you don't have to wait in line for the rides. You just enter through the exit and Bam! You are next in line for Pirates of the Caribbean, Bam! It's a Small World, Bam! Splash Mountain. No waiting! Talk about a Fast Pass.

All that day at Disneyland I indulged in the burn of envious stares from the straight families standing in hour-long lines who were probably thinking, "What the fuck's up the with the two faggots and a retard getting on without waiting in line?" I told Jojo to wave to all the people whenever the log or rocket or boat we were in was about to launch. I would egg him on, "Wave to all the voters of Prop 8, Jojo!" And he would comply. He'd wave his meaty man hand accompanied by a happy, goofy smile. I was loving it. Gregorio was a little irritated with my crassness, but he was also happy we were getting on all the rides, easily, quickly, nearing his childhood goal. I was doing a good job. I was being a good man, a good partner. We were all having a great, great time. Until the Parade of Dreams.

The fight that got Gregorio and me into therapy was exhausting and filled with lots of yelling. See, I'm a little bit scattered, especially in stressful situations. If too much is happening or too many people are talking, I have the brain capacity of a finch. Like many other people, I've locked my keys in the car, I've left my credit card at the gas station, and I've left the heater on as I exited the house, but something strange happened to me once I met Gregorio. My oversights increased and became much more significant throughout our years together. Because of me we've missed family functions, flights, and concerts. I once dropped Gregorio's iPhone into an airport urinal. I've accidentally sexted his grandmother. Once, I was using his computer without his permission and made one of those stupid click-click-click moves that wipe out hours of work in three seconds. Guau, I had never seen Gregorio so pissed. His blowup would've been sexy, but in his ranting he shouted at me, "Pendejo!" Simply, "Pendejo!" Now, pendejo is definitely not the strongest word in Spanish cuss vocabulary. There are, believe me, way worse words. But when your boyfriend looks you straight in the eye and, with ganas, with blood and bite in the word, calls you a pendejo. Well, I didn't know what to say or do. I didn't cry. But nearly.

So that one particular fight led to Ms. Shayla. Once in her office, Gregorio was calm and broke down his concerns in a quiet, intellectual way. He said that he wanted to take his life to the next level and he needed someone who was capable, someone who could keep up with him. He wanted a competent partner who was a man, not some scatterbrained, messy boy. He wanted a partner, not a burden. I think that actually hurt as much as his calling me pendejo. Ms. Shayla worked with us for a long while and, at times, pointed out all my competencies to Gregorio. She gave us exercises and homework to complete because, at that point, we still wanted to work together.

So there we were in front of Sleeping Beauty's Castle trying to find a seat for the Parade of Dreams. There were hordes of tense people standing around like they were all waiting for the next register at Costco to open up. However, unlike the rides, there is no special seating set aside for special people during parades unless you're in a wheelchair. Gregorio and I were absorbed in the task of locating an empty curb spot. Jojo kept tugging and grunting. He pulled my arm really hard. I don't think he knows how strong he is. I don't think he realizes he's a man. "That's it, were going to Jack-in-the-Box right now," I raised my voice at him, trying to imitate my aunt. And then I turned away to continue to look for an empty spot. I just didn't notice anything. There were so many moving people, and our goal was to get a good seat for the parade that was about to start. We were separated by just a few feet.

When I retraced my steps back to where Gregorio and Jojo had been, Gregorio was standing alone.

"I think I see a space over there," he said.

"Where's Jojo?" I answered back.

"I thought he went with you." The mad craning of our necks started simultaneously with the overbearing parade music. The fucking parade had started, and down the street came a well coordinated tsunami of animal herds and floats and men dressed as flamingos and manic dancers and sea creatures and princesses. It was like the gay apocalypse. Gregorio and I dashed to and fro calling out, "Jojo! Jojo! Jojo!"

We didn't leave the parking lot until about 3 a.m. Five more hours and it would have been a 24-hour trip to Disneyland. Jojo was knocked out in the backseat. A custodian had found him hiding in Mickey's Toontown. My aunt had been blowing up my cell phone since midnight. I kept asking Gregorio to tell her we were on our way, there was traffic, we were almost there, we were almost there. I finally sent her a picture of Jojo sleeping in the backseat just to calm her down. He looked like a drunk, passed-out homeless man.

Therapists say that transsexual little boys have a special affinity for Ariel, Disney's Little Mermaid, because her top half is female but her bottom half is ambiguous. I don't think I'm transsexual, but when Ms. Shayla asked me what I wanted from my relationship from Gregorio I thought of Ariel. In my head I saw Ariel in her secret cove surrounded by her clutter of thingamabobs, combing her hair with a fork, and singing about how she wanted to be part of the sailor's world, Eric the Human's world. That's what I want. I want to be part of Gregorio's world—the ordered, amusement-park life of fun, goal-oriented ambition. I don't know if I can swallow down my disqualifications, but I still want to scuba dive in Catalina, hunt Joshua trees in the desert, and visit a Palm Springs clothing-optional resort with my man, my dimpled hidrocalido with the long, long lashes. That is what I want. I love Gregorio.

We dropped off an extremely tired Jojo close to 4 a.m. He didn't even wave goodbye or say thank you when I told him goodnight. He just wanted to get to bed. I returned to the car, where Gregorio was waiting. He sat silently. He was very still but very, very wide awake. I wanted to say something but nothing came to my mind. Sorry was so puny and exhausted at that point. I was afraid to even turn on the radio. He stared out the window as if he was looking at something on the windshield. I could see the silhouette of his adorable camel eyelashes in profile, but definitely no dimple. He wouldn't turn his head toward me. He sat, motionless, in the passenger seat as I placed both of my hands on the steering wheel. I started the car, and we drove home together for the very last time.

Papua New Guinea Male Initiation Rites

I keep "nigger" ready in the holster of my back pocket because more blacks have called me faggot than whites. It is right next to my long machete of "¡chinga tu madre güey!" wielded against an equal number of potty-mouthed, soap-hungry wetbacks. Geographically, I'm usually ready to brandish the weapons after-hours outside seedy East Hollywood clubs or over loud, gum-speckled, nighttime streets, but this time I was in a library. I heart libraries. I particularly heart libraries that are old and spacious and as sacredly quiet as mosques and crammed with books the way thrift stores are crammed with clothes. Libraries are ordered universes of words that should be honored with silence and quiet steps, suppressed sneezes.

The two black teenagers had seated themselves in the middle of a row of four computer stations. I was using the computer on the end to search for a book of Pablo Neruda's poetry. Library patrons need a password to access Doheny Library's computers. I don't know how they had retrieved the password, but one of the teenagers was watching music videos and the other was playing an Internet video game. Although the dtoom-dtoom-dtoom-dtoom of the music video was muffled, it was also fucking irritating. The computers are set up high by design, meant to discourage standing users from staying too long. The teenagers, however, didn't mind sitting on low sofa chairs they had dislocated from a study lounge and pulled up close to the terminals. With his long arms raised above eye-level, the one playing the video game rapidly and loudly rattled the arrow buttons on the keyboard. Tat-tat-tat-tat-tat, the noise machine-gunned the Gothic serenity of the room. My inner, easily-annoyed Republican white lady, La Buffy Butterfield, began to get really irritated. Bad thoughts and bad words swelled in my heart into incendiary cuss poems.

I was looking for a particular book of Pablo Neruda's poetry. I had met this book of odes randomly, someone had abandoned it on one of the study tables a few months before. It looked like a lonely tree, on a wide prairie, wanting to be sat under. I had picked it up, perused the odes, and then decided to check the book out. The poems were in Spanish, but the book contained the best English marginalia I had ever read. Someone very learned had penciled in various notes and references to the poems and offered some unusually precise English translations. I didn't remember the title of the book, but I needed that particular copy because of its penciled-in marginalia. At work I was leading a lesson on anthropomorphizing objects. I was teaching fourth graders how to use metaphors. I wanted to demonstrate how poets had been making candlesticks dance and teapots sing way before Disney cartoons. I thought of Neruda and his "Ode to an Artichoke" as a beautiful, perfect example of what I wanted my students to learn. And it was bilingual to boot. They could receive the lesson in two languages, in linguistic stereo. But when I typed "Neruda" into the digitized library catalog I got 1,689 results. Maybe it was more that avalanche of results that made me irritated than the noisy teenagers themselves.

But at that point it didn't matter, because La Buffy Butterfield suddenly manifested herself. A small, 40-something-ish librarian scurried into where we all were and began laying into the boys: "I already told you guys you can't use these computers for video games. Am I going to have to call security? Do you want to be banned from campus? Wah wah wah, wah wah wah." And although I was really glad she showed up, I was also really glad I was never going to marry a woman because she had that archetypal banshee tone of voice that grates the ears of all mammalian males regardless of sexual preference. The shrieks were effective, don't get me wrong, but I immediately felt for all of the reprimanded husbands of the world who had forgotten to take out the trash. The black teenagers, with wide grins, logged off, jumped up, and moved the sofas back to their proper places in one swift dance as if the scene had all been choreographed beforehand. They scurried away in separate directions. They laughed derisively at the white lady, but she had got them up off the computers. I think she knew and they knew that she would never really call campus security. We all knew Doheny Library had three things their homes probably didn't have: air conditioning, high-speed Internet, and silence.

Doheny Library is in the middle of USC's campus and USC's campus is in the middle of a ghetto and the ghetto is south of downtown of the second-largest city in the United States, which itself was in the middle of a summer heat wave. The library was refreshingly cool and empty, except for a few bored employees, two neighborhood boys, and me.

I myself had understood and loved the sanctuary libraries provide since my East LA nerd-kid days, when I would spend summers sequestered at the Anthony Quinn branch. That branch library was the best place to cool off, and the safest place to browse through the anthropology and the oversized art-book section. It is in those sections that 10-year-olds learn that libraries cultivate the talent of looking through books to find pictures of naked men. This is accomplished by introducing boys to Robert Mapplethorpe photography and pictures of Papua New Guinea male initiation rites. Boys learn the code words that mean men with no clothes. Libraries were never, ever boring.

During undergraduate studies I worked at the main university research library at UCLA. I was employed there during the 1994 Northridge earthquake that felled a million books from the shelves. All of the undergrads who worked at the library had to put in 10-hour shifts for two weeks in order to re-shelve all the fallen books and get the library back in working order. All five floors had piles of books nearly waist deep.

My co-worker and section partner then was Christine. We had to re-shelve the Physical Science section. Rows of heavy, thick, broad-back-ed books. Christine was a Coptic Christian who looked more Latina than Middle Eastern. She was one of the Christians of Egypt who tattoo themselves in religious devotion. She was dark-haired, olive-skinned and had frilly crucifixes tattooed on the insides of both her wrists. She had received the tattoos when she was 9. She looked like a sacred chola, pretty but intense. She was dating this big-nosed, hairy-armed Muslim guy. They had a closeted relationship because of their differing religions. Their family and friends would have strongly disapproved. A discovery would have been grounds for Christine's removal from school, she confided to me. School was her sanctuary, the library her safe house. So big-nosed Ali had to visit Christine at her job at the library in order to steal kisses and conversations. They would take long lunch hours together, canoodling in the sculpture garden adjacent to the building.

One time, after they had walked back from lunch, I looked through that space books create between their tops and the bottoms of the shelves above them. It's the small crevice that is narrow but really, really deep, like a crack into the Earth. I looked through the crack when I heard a noise some shelves over. I saw Ali kissing Christine. She had wrapped her crucifix-stamped wrists around his hairy neck. She looked like she was hanging from him. I couldn't see her face, but I could tell she was happy.

The computer wasn't any help in finding the title or location of that Neruda book, so I decided just to take my chances and peruse the poetry section of Doheny. The section was on the bottom floor, deep underground. As I exited the creaky, jumpy elevator the entire floor was absorbed in the overwhelming hum of an antiquated ventilation system. It sounded like the letter *n* was stuck in the air: NNNNNNNN.

As I got off, a janitor lady pushed her clunky, yellow cleaning cart into the elevator. She was going up. I smiled "buenas tardes" to her, and she returned the pleasantry. I then quickly located the poetry section and started to search for the Neruda book, which, surprisingly, wasn't difficult to find after all. I had only remembered the lime-green spine of the book when I saw it again, blaring from a bottom shelf. It was as if the book were waiting for me. I checked to make sure the penciled marginalia were still there, and they were. As I slammed the book shut in satisfaction, I looked up to see one of the teenage boys, the one who had been watching the dtoom-dtoom-dtoom music video. He was sitting on the desk of one of the enclosed study stalls waaaaay down across the other side of the narrow canyon of books that I was standing in, nearly on the other side of the building. I could only see his shoulders and head. He had been watching me talk to myself, watching me smile and laugh at finding the book like I was some happy, insane person discovering a leprechaun. He surprised me. We stared at each other. He chucked his head up at me like I was supposed to catch his chin. Then he stood up, assured. It was then that I saw the Mapplethorpe, his Papua New Guinea sticking out of his pants. The hum of the ventilation system grew louder. NNNNNNNN.

I could smell on him that it had been hot outside and that he had walked a few blocks to get here. It was his warm sudor that was flavored not only with today's temperature but also with a genealogy of Creole ancestors, hip-hop tics, and restless bravado. My mustache crunched up against his coarse curlicues. He was really rough the way young men are. I was really patient the way good teachers are. He kept saying, "Yeah nigga', yeah nigga'." My over-thinking mind was trying to figure out if he was referring to himself in the third person singular, or if he was talking about me in the second person. But the grammarian debate in me soon was overwhelmed with needed attention to the mechanics of swallowing.

There are really no differences between animals, people, and things, I told my fourth graders. On an atomic level, we are all alive. Everything is alive. Rocks, books, vegetables, insects, us. The job of metaphors and of poets is to remind us of that connected aliveness. Everybody responds to that truth if it is pointed out to them in a convincing and beautiful way.

As an example, I told my students that when I was photocopying the poem from the book at the library for them, the janitor lady was sweeping the floor of the copy room. We started talking. She was from El Salvador. I asked her if she wanted to hear some poetry, from Chile, from Neruda. She said: "Claro. Soy bruta pero aqui 'stoy con mis orejas limpias." I turned toward her with the open book and began to read the ode aloud like it was some ambush poetry reading. It was just she and I in the copy room suddenly filled with this loud ode. I saw her reveal her silver-lined teeth as I got to the end, the part where the artichoke is cooked and then eaten:

> *así termina*
>
> *en paz*
>
> *esta carrera*
>
> *del vegetal armado*
>
> *que se llama alcachofa,*
>
> *luego*
>
> *escama por escama*
>
> *desvestimos*
>
> *la delicia*
>
> *y comemos*
>
> *la pacifica pasta*
>
> *de su corazón verde.* *

She smiled. And I smiled. And we clapped and laughed at the poem's perfection. We clapped at the happiness of Spanish. She said, nodding her head, "Yes, it's true, it's true artichokes have soft hearts just like we have soft hearts." So after hearing the anecdote and my reading of the poem in class, the kids clapped, too, because they understood what I was teaching.

When I exited Doheny library with my photocopies in hand, I saw the two black teenagers outside planning, conversing, arguing over how they were to divvy up their $3 once they got to Taco Bell. They had skateboards and tilted baseball hats and a restlessness hanging on them like too many clothes. I stared at them. At him. Maybe too long. Until the other one interrupted,

"What you looking at, Faggot?" he shouted.

A chain of curses curled up in my mouth like a ball of magician's handkerchiefs tied to one another; they filled my mouth wanting to be pulled out, one right behind another, a bright red "fuck you," followed by a polka-dot purple "nigger." But I looked at the other boy, and instead of a handkerchief-filled mouth magician I became a sword swallower, like those performers who take samurai swords down in slow, careful gulps. I looked at the one who had been listening to the dtoom-dtoom-dtoom music, the one who had been screamed at by a white lady librarian, the one whose house was too hot and too loud, the one who smelled like a heat wave, Louisiana, hip-hop, and bravado. He looked down at his skateboard. I heard the broken-down sound of the old ventilation system egging me on, NNNNNNNN.

"Nothing," I said. "I'm not looking at nothing."

They plopped down their skateboards with loud, irritating cracks and rolled away.

*Neruda, Pablo, "Oda a la alcachofa"

Chicano Studies

The Mexican pilot barely offered us enough notice. The stewardesses were already zooming up the aisles, hunched over, urgently spritzing insecticide by our seats as the plane descended into Havana's José Martí International. Before the pilot had finished announcing what the women were doing, the women were done. We had no opportunity to object, or decline; to raise our hands and ask ... um ... why exactly did the airline need to spray pesticide in the cabin before we landed? Was it cucarachas? Capitalism? What stowaway aboard a flight from Mexico City to the Cuban capital warranted an ambush fumigation ... or maybe it was all a trick. Maybe it was a ploy to provoke and, thus, identify two American schoolteachers on a vacation dare. Because only Americans, coddled by slippery-when-wet signs, suggestion boxes, democracy, and the-customer-is-always-right bullshit, would think to challenge the way something is done in other countries.

As my anxiety grew, I tried to imagine the mutiny that would foment if an American stewardess, shaking a can of Raid, let loose on an inbound flight to LAX or JFK. Why wasn't anyone saying anything? In any cultural context, the surprise fumigation just didn't seem right. But what could I do? Neither Mexico nor Cuba were my countries. Shut up and be grateful the pilot even said anything, I told myself. Ms. Garcia, my colleague and travel companion, just gave a shrug when she saw my quizzical, questioning look; then she peered out the window at the island city zooming in like Google Earth, but over a slow connection. She seemed more excited about our arrival than concerned with the well-being of her lungs. "It's so shiny in all that sun," she said, and made sure to secure her baseball cap, which had a manic-looking Mickey Mouse emblazoned on the front.

"Why did you bring that tacky cap?" I asked.

"It's all I had; I don't want my face to get dark," she said.

"It's already dark."

"Shut up," she responded. I looked away from her, back into the aisle, wondering if I could hold my breath until we reached our gate and disembarked onto the embargoed isle.

Ms. Garcia and I had a blast in Cuba, of course. We partied like white kids on spring break. We both met scrumptious Cuban men, men who couldn't get fat or stalk you back to your home country even if they wanted to. Isaac and Ramsis served as competent, amorous tour guides. Ms. Garcia and I played brown-sugar mama and brown-sugar daddy, respectively. Together, we all swam and splashed at each other in the warm Gulf of Mexico, ate homemade comida criolla, snapped a bunch of pictures by The Boat, danced at la Casa de la Musica, and visited a santero who looked into us and made Ms. Garcia cry. He was the only Cuban who left us with a bad feeling.

Isaac, Ms. Garica's tour guide/vacation lover, warned us not to speak as he hailed a decrepit '58 Chevy Impala because locals could get in trouble if they offered rides to tourists. Ms. Garcia and I could pass as cubanos if we didn't open our mouths, Isaac said. "But then who ever heard of a quiet Cuban?" Ramsis rebutted. We laughed as Ramsis and I hunkered into the back seat once the illegal cab had stopped to pick us all up. When Ms. Garcia slipped into the passenger seat after Isaac she exerted too much fuerza to make sure she securely closed the heavy door. When it slammed, the driver yelled, "Coño, are you fucking American?" Our cover was nearly blown by Ms. Garcia's biceps. I didn't know we were known for slamming car doors. Isaac interceded and smoothed over our not-really-a-taxi taxi-driver by paying him the fare up front.

Our ride ended in front of an old crumbling building on Aguacate Street.

Isaac led us into one room and then another until we met an old man whom we paid some respectful saludos and some crinkled dollars. There were five of us huddled in a tiny, candlelit space. As the experience got creepier, I used a sideways glance to remind Ms. Garcia this had been all her idea. The old man smoked a stinky cigar, swished some rum in his mouth, and invoked his ancient African gods dressed in Catholic drag. His eyes rolled back into his head, looked at his brain, and then his pupils returned into view in between rapid eyelid flutters. As he spoke he seemed to focus his intensity on Ms. Garcia. I felt ignored but remained reverent, trying to keep up with his speedy, sing-song Spanish. He spoke mostly of Ms. Garcia's long-dead father. She got serious, then weepy. I tried to act patient and interested. Then he looked at me, and then back at both of us and quickly added, almost as a throwaway, "Mija, cuidado con los hombres que pasan por tu vida." Then he abruptly stopped talking and remained silent. Isaac said that was our sign to leave. I was, like: "What does that all mean? Was he talking about me? I don't understand. What just happened?" Everyone ignored my questions because Ms. Garcia was still crying after having been assured by the old cubano that her dead father loved her and hadn't meant to die so early.

She didn't seem to care about the cryptic warning concerning the men she spends her life with and the insinuating glance toward me. By then, my impatience and my stomach had taken over. "I'm hungry," I told a distracted, long-faced Ms. Garcia as we all stood outside the old cubano's building. "I want to go now. I want to be by myself, with Ramsis." I looked at the good-looking, smiling Ramsis. Ms. Garcia agreed and turned one way down Aguacate Street with her man while I turned the other with mine.

On our last day in Havana, Ms. Garcia and I went to something of a makeshift marketplace. We were reviewing and philosophizing about our wonderful trip and deciding where we should travel upon our return to Mexico. Veracruz? Oaxaca? Cancún? Then I brought up the santero experience. "Are you cool now?" I asked. "Do you feel better?"

"Yeah, I do," she answered, "Isaac and I had a good, long talk afterward."

"I bet you did," I said, then added, "Do you believe all that woo-woo santería?"

"I believe my dad loved me."

"What about what the santero said about us?"

"He said something about us?" she looked at me, not remembering.

"Berets!" I shouted uncontrollably as I looked past her not-remembering face. I spotted a display of handmade berets behind Ms. Garcia and could not hold back my distracted enthusiasm. What a perfect souvenir! Kitschy, communist, cool. The hats all had commie red stars sewn into the middle just like Che Guevara's. A synchronistic inspiration struck: I knew then and there on that Havana street corner in midsummer what I would be for the fall's Halloween parade at Babylon Street Elementary!

After bartering for the beret, we walked over to Havana's Malecón. I was happy thinking about the fall. Ms. Garcia was still in Cuba. She pointed out a young guy with long hair, light skin and green eyes sitting by a blanket where he displayed his wares for sale as if he were on Venice Beach in California. He looked like a bored rockero. He was selling handmade wooden key chains with ¡Viva Cuba! painted on them. They looked like they would fall apart if they got wet or if you grabbed your keys too tightly. Ms. Garcia stared at this handsome young guy selling the cheap tchotchkes and said, in English, "Sometimes I just want to give this country a big hug." The rockero looked exhausted with island fever, while the key chains seemed like projects made on craft day in an insane asylum.

"You know what Isaac told me yesterday?" Ms. Garcia went on. "Since he can never go see the world, he can at least appreciate when the world comes sees him. Then he gave me a kiss on my forehead."

She was getting sentimental, maybe even falling in love. "Girl, I'm glad we're leaving tomorrow," I told her. "It's none too soon for you." I didn't tell her I'd let Ramsis have my Levi's, my travel soaps, and the silver-plated bracelet we'd each bought one of when Ms. Garcia and I were in Taxco, Guerrero.

We tied up the last three weeks of our summer vacation in Guanajuato,

Mexico, and when we returned to LA it was still August, so I had plenty of time to finish the scavenger hunt that the making of my costume had become. The imported communist beret was the first piece.

Ever since I was little my mom, the homemaker-seamstress-wizard, had helped her three children create their Halloween costumes from inspirations prompted by something as simple as a television commercial or a coloring book. Nothing demonstrated the pulsating mother-love of our household as well as my daily slicked-back head of hair, antipyretic pots of caldito de pollo, and the family's annual sweep of the Halloween parade prizes. My outfits had never been purchased on aisle 10 of some random supermarket ransacked on October 30.

Halloween was always well planned and appropriately feted. However, after I had grown up and graduated from UCLA with a degree in Chicano studies, the world became much more serious. Eating beans, hitting piñatas, dating, even celebrating Halloween became opportunities to use my degree in efforts to help dismantle White Capitalist Imperialist Patriarchy.

My goal every Halloween became to dress as "something Chicano." My outfits *always* had to reference my Mexican-American ethnicity. This proved fun but challenging. By my fifth Halloween, I had already exhausted my decorative sombrero with the usual suspects – Emiliano Zapata, Pancho Villa, a mariachi, a Posada-inspired calavera. Unless I was willing to do Chicano drag, I was running out of ideas.

Then came our visit to Ms. Garcia's home city of Guadalajara during our summer tour of Mexico. As we slurped our liquados in the local mall, she surprised me with a sudden double dare, "Let's go to Cuba." She stared at me with wide happy eyes and a traviesa smile.

I love this girl, is what I first thought. I smiled "yes" back at her, and 45 minutes later we had purchased our tickets.

I knew Che wasn't mexicano, but then again, he wasn't even cubano. He and Fidel Castro, however, had rendezvoused in Mexico. And it was from Tuxpan, Veracruz, that their infamous 1956 yacht ride to you-know-where had started. The connection was tenuous, yes, but just Chicano enough for my Halloween.

When Ms. Garcia and I traveled to Havana via Mexico, there were two things (besides the surprise fumigation) that struck me immediately as we made it to the city. The first was that everyone was black. Despite my ethnic-studies education, I honestly had not known about this beforehand. I got off the plane and thought the airport looked like an underfunded post office in 1980s Compton until I heard all the black people speaking Spanish. It was disorienting, but obviously consciousness-raising, as any good trip should be. Gloria Estefan, Ricky Ricardo, and Elián González had really fucked with my perception of the island and the color of its people. I always thought Celia Cruz, bless her soul, was some Australian Aborigine anomaly. The second thing I noticed, as we drove into the city, was that there were only two types of advertisements allowed – those pertaining to *The Revolution;* and those presenting the United States as the epitome of evil, the Skeletor, the Lord Voldermort of nations. The main spokesperson in ads about *The Revolution* was none other than the handsome, beret-ed Che Guevara.

On that last day, when I looked past Ms. Garcia to the berets being sold on that street corner, I excitedly approached the vendor who, in turn, began to barter with me for Ms. Garcia's beige, Mickey Mouse-emblazoned baseball cap. The tacky cotton cap was the kind easily acquired at any mall cart or thrift-store bin in the United States, but in Havana the hat turned out to be akin in desirability to a rowboat and a couple of oars. Every passerby noticed the hat as if it had been a bonnet of gold. Ms. Garcia was pestered for it wherever we walked. Seeing how much I wanted the beret, my good friend offered the beret peddler her sun protection in trade so that I could possess the first element of my next Halloween costume.

Back in LA I acquired military boots, fatigues, and a black wig in the attempt to replicate Che Guevara's 1960s guerilla-rebel aesthetic. However, when I tried the wig on with the beret, I looked more like an illegal immigrant from Mexico in the 1970s. It was not the dashing revolutionary look I was going for. I had this schizophrenic debate about whether to wear the wig or not. But realism won out. Referring to Alberto Korda's famous photo of Che that showed the dude with lots of hair hanging from his star-studded beret, looking more like a halo than a hat, I surrendered to authenticity, stapled the damn wig to the beret, and donned the headpiece.

The other problem I knew I would have on Halloween, particularly during the day at Babylon Elementary, was explaining my costume to my second graders. I tried to persuade Ms. Garcia to dress as Tania the Guerrilla in order to help me educate my students about revolutionaries. "Who the hell is Tania the Guerilla?" she asked.

"She was an Argentinean spy who helped Che wage his Bolivian campaign."

"You're crazy! I'm not dressing as that. I've already planned on being Little Bo Peep for my kindergartners."

"Bo-ring."

"At least people will know who I am," she insisted. "No one ever even knows who you dress as. Why can't you just be a cowboy or pirate or something like that? You can dress as one of Little Bo Peep's sheep!"

"More like a sheep to White Capitalist Imperialist Patriarchy."

"Whatever, Tony."

But she was right. I knew I could expect the whiny questioning of 7-year-olds: "Mr. Villalobos, what are you? I don't get it. What are you supposed to be? What are you dressed as? Tell us. Tell us." I tried to use my costumes as catalysts for memorable, teachable moments, but explaining revolutionary figures to children in primary school doesn't really work, no matter how you attempt to translate neocolonialism into kid language. I've tried. If I just told them I was a solider, the answer would shut them up but miss the whole point of the costume.

Being a teacher at a poor, inner-city school with a student population that is 99.8 percent immigrant Latino, I discovered how at Halloween you have to navigate the landmines of parental neglect, student embarrassment, and cultural misunderstanding. At Babylon Street Elementary, October

31 meant the sudden infusion of dark little indigenous girls looking like Mexico City transvestites in crooked blond wigs and taffeta Disney ballgowns. It meant chubby Mayan-boy Darth Vaders. It meant little round brown kids trying to insert themselves into the square holes of American pop culture. Our school's Halloween parade always reminded me of the legend of the Tehuantepec women taking the petticoats from a European shipwreck and, thinking they were headdresses, putting them up on their heads. It was definitely a day bursting with *National Geographic*-type photo opportunities.

Most of the children at my school are the first in their families to actually celebrate Halloween. The Che Guevara year, it was Stephanie who confounded our class with her concoction. This unfortunate little girl, the heftiest one in the class, already had the cards stacked against her. She was fat, smelly, unkempt, and, earlier in the year, had gained infamy among her classmates by unwittingly transporting, from her home to school, a nest of roaches in her backpack. Stephanie was already an outcast and only solidified her designation as such after this particular Halloween. Her mom didn't get the whole Halloween idea; the immigrant woman barely understood the benefit of clean clothes or the concept of homework. She had sent Stephanie to school with a costume carelessly crumpled into a plastic bag from Vons supermarket. When Stephanie saw all the other little girls already dressed and primped as princesses and cute witches, she urgently asked me if she could go change into her costume. I let her. When she returned from the restroom she was wearing this strange, funky, dress-like construction that, randomly, had one of Roy Lichtenstein's pieces of art imprinted upon it. The hem culminated in dramatic wavy curves held up by wire. It was as if she were wearing really bad conceptual art. I didn't get it. She walked back into the classroom sheepishly. I tried to ignore her so as not to draw attention and face the inevitable, unanswerable question that I knew would be asked. But, *of course*, loud-mouthed Joseph began his interrogation. "What is she? What are you, Stephanie? Mr. Villalobos, what is she supposed be?" I didn't know what the fuck she was. At Joseph's questioning, all the students turned toward her. Stephanie just stood quietly and bit her tiny fist, embarrassed, scanning all the children who were looking at her and her outfit. She, herself, was completely unsure of what she was supposed to be. *I* couldn't even *guess* what she was. My best answer would have been, "She's a Roy Lichtenstein." But I knew that would not have been a satisfactory answer, just as answering "I'm Emiliano Zapata" or "I'm Che Guevara" would never have satisfied a second grader curious about who I was dressed as. So I just did what teachers do when they can't answer a question—"Joseph, I'm not answering your question because you didn't raise your hand." To spare Stephanie, I quickly changed the subject while she shuffled to her seat and tried to figure how to sit down with that stiff, curvy hemline. I wanted to make her therapy-in-the-making moment as minimally traumatic as it could be. That year, the year I dressed as the beret-ed Che and Stephanie, a Roy Lichtenstein-something-or-other, was the year I met Jason.

Later on that night, Ms. Garcia and I went to West Hollywood. She skillfully transformed her costume from Little Bo Peep into Little Ho' Peep. Suddenly, after work, her shepherdess cleavage plunged, and her frilly skirt rose high enough to reveal tempting garters and white stilettos. I made alterations to my costume, too.

In order to make the point and reduce the confusion as to who I was, and to avoid an adult version of Stephanie's embarrassment, I decided to download the famous Korda photo, print it on iron-on paper, iron the image onto the back of my costume, and then write the name Che across the image in leftover glitter glue just to drive home the point. I was sure many, many people had seen this internationally known photo, or at least a corruption of it. But of course, because knowledge of history, just like knowledge of geography or one's congressional representative, is knowledge not widely valued or indulged in, there was more than one occasion while walking down a crowded Santa Monica Boulevard that night when drunken teams of teenagers would approach me and say something like: "Oh, look how cool! It's that guy ... that guy ... um ... César Chávez!" And then they'd ask if they could pose for a picture with César Chávez. As I posed with them I was thinking: "I'm not fucking César Chávez! When did César Chávez ever wear a goddamn beret?! He was a nonviolent farmworker organizer. How would anyone dress up as César Chávez anyway? Wear a plaid shirt and not eat for a week?" This only proved the desperate need for more Chicano studies classes in public schools.

As we walked down Santa Monica Boulevard that night we saw Stormtroopers, Adam and Eve, and cheerleaders with facial hair and broad backs. The cow that jumped over the moon was there, and so was a well-put-together, bloody Tipi Hedron from Hitchcock's *The Birds*. But my favorite costume stood in the middle of a commotion. It was Alien from the 1979 movie *Alien*.

He could barely walk down the street. So many people were stopping him and posing for pictures; the costume was very realistic. I stopped him, too, and we posed for a very postmodern photograph of Alien strangling Che Guevara a.k.a. César Chávez. However, as he took his alien clutches away from my neck, his costume's limb caught my wig, and both my long hair and my Cuban beret flew off my head. He started apologizing profusely and tried to pick up my hair with his claws. I said it was alright. We both reached for the fallen beret at the same time. It was all, suddenly, very romantic. I saw one human eye look at me through an extraterrestrial nostril. He complimented my costume and correctly identified me as Che. Then he asked my name. I *knew* I looked better without long hair. Now, I could not see this guy, just his eye, but he was nice enough (I set the bar pretty low on nights when all the men in West Hollywood are dressed as aliens or women). We chatted a while and he asked for my number. People kept interrupting our conversation to pose for photographs with him, so I cut our chat short and called his cell as a way to record my number. As Ms. Garcia looked on, Alien looked at her and then asked, "Who are you dressed as?" I teased her all the way back to our cars.

It turns out Alien's name was Jason and he was this white guy. I wasn't too attracted to him once he removed his ectoskeleton. Nevertheless, we attempted to kiss and date and connect, but it never worked out. He worked in movie make-up. He had tons of costumes, masks and access to high-quality special-effects materials. His apartment was adorned with plastic guts and decapitated heads. We became friends, and the following year I asked if I could borrow his Alien costume. Now I knew I was not going to be abiding strictly to my own royal proclamation concerning Chicano costumes, but if any smartass challenged my commitment to El Movimiento I was going to claim I was dressed as an illegal alien. Jason's Alien costume was so realistic and professional, made with spandex and rubber and foam and love of detail, I just couldn't pass up my access to it. It was going to be a hit at my school! The thing was, I couldn't dress as the Alien before I arrived at work because I had to drive myself there and unload a bunch of Halloween party supplies once I parked. So just like fat, smelly Stephanie the previous year, Mr. Villalobos had to arrive out of costume and transport it in canvas shopping bags from Whole Foods.

The year I borrowed Jason's Alien suit, Ms. Garcia was a kitten. She dressed all in black, wore a headband with triangular ears, painted whiskers on her cheeks, and attached a tail to her butt.

Also that year I had an English-only class filled mostly with precocious boys and daring girls who were very familiar with Halloween, much more assimilated than most of the other students at the school. They were already 7-year-old badasses often discussing Chucky and Jigsaw and the new pantheon of horror-film characters as if they were Saturday morning cartoons. My students often took pleasure in filling me in on the plots and characters of the R-rated *Saw IV* or *The Hills Have Eyes*. They pleaded with me to read scary stories instead of our basal readers, and to decorate the class jack-o-lanterns with fake blood. Once Halloween week rolled around I told them what I was going to be and they couldn't wait to see it. I even sneaked in snippets of the *Alien* sequel, my favorite, just to entice them. I realized then that the film had been made *decades* before they were born. It held up pretty well, however. I made sure to include the footage of the Latina bulldyke character Vasquez, you know, just to subvert white heterosexual hegemony in the way we Chicano studies majors like to do it. That Halloween day, I put on the costume in front of them, with the help of my teacher's aide Stacy, and they thought I was the coolest Alien teacher ever. Score, Mr. Villalobos. We all posed for pictures taken with the school's digital camera and titled the images *Alien Massacres the Second Grade* and *Alien Wins at Tetherball* and *Alien Can't Read 90 Words per Minute*. After our photo shoot we had to get ready for the school-wide parade.

Ms. Garcia taught kindergarten right next door to me. We had conjoining classrooms. We shared a door. I don't know what I was thinking. I think my class of little badasses got me carried away with the holiday spirit. I mean, I knew my costume was scary, but it was Halloween after all. That's the point, right? I didn't think it could get out of hand. I didn't want to hurt anybody. I honestly didn't think it through. It was all supposed to be fun. I was having so much fun up to that point. It was a spur-of-the-moment decision.

I had volunteered my class to help set up for the parade on the playground, so they all left with Stacy to arrange chairs and hang orange streamers. While I put the finishing touches on my costume, slipping on the claws, I could hear the kindergartners settling in next door in Ms. Garcia's class. I was alone in my classroom and I could hear her gathering the kids onto the rug for their next lesson. When I peaked through the clear glass of the fire extinguisher case, which our rooms shared, I could see the kindergartners moving to their places on the rug—cute midgets shuffling around in bright, tiny costumes coordinated by a tall, pretty kitty cat. When they finally all settled down and a quiet lull arose, I struck. I swung open the door like a swat team officer, and with my long alien limbs raised to the ceiling I launched myself into the room with a huge, extraterrestrial ...

..."ROOOOOAR!"

I was louder than even I expected to be. I didn't even know I was capable of roaring like that. You know how they say in moments of panic or emergency people will revert to their instinctual fight-or-flight response. Well, I would say most of those kids had a flight response because nearly all jumped up so fast their swiftness took me by surprise. They screamed in unison as if it had been an earthquake or terrorist attack. Nearly all fled toward the front door or behind Ms. Garcia. Some did strange hysterics like running in place or hitting others really close to them. It was a really strange sight. Very primal. Even Ms. Garcia flinched out of her chair. I would've laughed, but the only one who didn't move from her place was a little, little ballerina who sat closest to the door conjoining our classrooms.

She was by my foot-claw. She sat crossed-legged on the floor wearing a pink leotard and a frilly tutu and a little tiara, her hair set in a neat, hairsprayed chongo that I'm sure her mother had taken all morning to twist. All the color had flushed from her glittered face, and a puddle of pee expanded from underneath her. I had never seen eyes so liquid and contracted, her mouth a cavernous frown. She didn't make one sound or even try to move out of the way. But she was vibrating, as if she were stuck in the air and couldn't get out.

Ms. Garcia looked at me in disbelief. I slouched and began to spit apologies. I couldn't immediately rip off the costume because the parts were too intricately attached to my own body; my claws were trembling and clumsy. I needed the assistance of my aide Stacy. There was all this sad whimpering in the room. I just keep saying: "It's me! ¡Soy yo! It's me! ¡El maestro Villalobos. Maestro Villalobos! No se preocupen. Lo siento. I'm sorry. I'm sorry." Ms. Garcia screamed at me to leave, she said I was making everything worse. It was exactly like the moment in the movie sequel when Sigourney Weaver tells the ugly Alien queen, who has a little girl in her sights, "Get away from her, you bitch!" Unfortunately, I was the bitch.

The little ballerina never returned to school. I heard she never completed kindergarten. The grade is not mandatory in California anyways—not that that makes the situation better. It's just a fact. The African-American woman who is our school psychologist asked me to explain a susto. She had spoken with the little ballerina's parents, who kept saying that she had a susto, and the psychologist didn't know what they meant. I loosely translated it as "a fear" that, in our culture, I suppose, is clinically akin to post traumatic stress syndrome. I guess that is one way to explain it, except that with a susto you need to drink special teas or visit a sobadora to get rid of it. The psychologist didn't really understand. She called it folklore. She said the girl wouldn't talk anymore. She called that selective mutism.

Ms. Garcia isn't mad at me, but she doesn't treat me the same. When I invite her out dancing or for happy hour at El Sombrero she's always busy now. It's been three years since our trip to the mall in Guadalajara when she asked me if I wanted to go to Cuba and do something that, as Americans, we weren't supposed to do. I remember her traviesa smile and all the fun we had.

The Halloween parade went well except that Ms. Garcia's class didn't participate. They were too traumatized. They stayed cooped up in their classroom. The guilt kept me quiet and serious for the rest of the day. As the school of brown Supermen and brunette Sleeping Beauties marched passed me, I thought of the legend of the Tehuanas: A chest stuffed with white petticoats handsewn in a Madrid convent or a Parisian home or a Dutch shop was loaded onto a Spanish galleon where it sat as cargo for months and months crossing a 17th-century ocean, traveling round the bottom of a new continent, near an ice world and then though a New World ocean until a hurricane, or a mutiny maybe, or an attack by English piratas interrupted the voyage and sank the ship. A confetti of flotsam was released over ocean leagues, including, floating amongst dead sailors and wood planks, the chest. A chest that bobbed in the ocean and washed up on the isthmus of Tehuantepec in Mexico. Dark indigenas, Tehuanas, found this wet chest, popped it open and were surprised by an explosion of petticoats, white and extraterrestrial. The women quizzically inspected the booty, then lugged the chest to their village where, after months or years of imagination and tinkering, they transformed the cloth into the resplandor, the huipil grande, the halo-like headdresses they loved so much.

Mission Girls

Sarahi was a gingerbread boy trapped inside a little half-Mexican, half-Guatemalan, all-American girl. She was in my kindergarten class four years ago when I taught kindergarten. She was the only Attention Deficit Hyperactivity Disorder girl I ever had as a student. Ninety-nine percent of the time, it was boys who could not sit still or who would "put-put-put-put-put-put" with their mouths until I wanted to demand, "Stop fucking with your mouth!" But I had come to understand that most of the ADHD-ers, male or female, just could not help moving, twitching, jerking their shoulders to some unheard beat, their bodies cursed, as in a fairy tale, with the inability to stop their boogie. Their purpose in life was to cultivate the compassion of their caregivers via wiggles. This time the afflicted was a little brown girl with sleepy eyes and thick everywhere hair, ADHD Sarahi. I felt bad for her. She wasn't mean or malicious, just painfully, fitfully restless. So I let her move around and touch things and twist into what seemed to be Hatha yoga postures as I taught. I just ignored her constant contortions until the other kids in the class learned to do the same thing. I think her classmates realized that it must have been pretty painful not to be able to sit still or wait your turn or concentrate on details like the capitalization of *i* when it stands alone. What was apparent, even to the other 5-year-olds, was that Sarahi had something inside her that she could not completely control; I imagined a kinetic gingerbread boy. Our class always ignored Sarahi's twirling and twitching until she would twirl and twitch into a situation we just couldn't ignore.

One day I had my garden of children laid out before me in their ordered rows and columns of attention, with ADHD Sarahi sitting in the first row, at the very end, surrounded by the smallest possible number of classmates. She sat in close proximity to nobody but me. While everybody else sat in lotus position, she moved from downward dog into warrior stance, then into plough all in the span of five seconds; it was her usual asanas-on-crack routine. I was saying something extremely important about the letter *H* as her busybody hands wrapped around the legs of a heavy, wooden easel I used to display the alphabet. She was grabbing the legs and pulling and pushing them as if she were trying to transfer her excessive energy off onto the peacefully still object, her psyche jealous of all stationary furniture. As I rambled on, accustomed to her bouncy vibrancy, everyone but her rapt in attention, everyone but her listening to me deconstruct the architecture of the letter *H*, BAM! the shit fell on her. There were two seconds of complete stillness in the class. Everyone had flinched, then frozen to the sudden sound of something like a porthole to another dimension cracking open in our classroom.

The otherworldly BAM! had opened up our attention. Sarahi moved out from under the fallen easel like a slinky cat. She was uninjured but shocked. She had that wide-eyed, what-the-fuck-just-happened look.

I started laughing and then, trying to switch into anger, I went into Latino parent mode: "Ves. Ves. I told you you move too much! You touch too many things!" I followed this up with the unconstitutional, "God punished you so you could learn." I had told her many, many times not to touch the damned easel. Now, because she hadn't listened, I felt I to had to evoke the God of the Red Sea, the Flood, and smoldering Gomorrah. She looked at me with big repentant eyes, still trying to figure out just what exactly had happened. She looked like a cartoon character wondering, "Where exactly did that anvil come from?" I picked her up and gave her a hug, trying to make up for my laughter and my attempt at amateur Catholic excommunication. I asked her if she was okay. She nodded yes while making the plumpest pucheros I had ever seen, while her eyes just then melted onto her cheeks.

In kindergarten you sometimes need to pick kids up and smother them with hugs even if it is against the rules or the error was their own *estupid* fault.

That was four years ago, when she was fun size, when she was a little gingerbread boy inside of a half-Mexican, half-Guatemalan, all-American girl. Both she and I are in fourth grade now, and four years later, both Sarahi and I are sitting in the principal's office waiting for the police to arrive as she cries and cries and cries, inconsolable and in really deep shit.

Even after the easel had let Sarahi have it, none of my Mexican Roman Catholic holy admonitions stopped her from moving too much or touching too many things. But at least she didn't mess with classroom furniture anymore. Although she stopped molesting the larger items, rulers, crayons, markers, scissors, and glue bottles couldn't defend themselves from mutilation like the top-heavy easel had. She avoided the chalkboard and, most importantly, my large, old-school, off-limits teacher desk because she was probably worried that either one could have bent over and slapped her if she got too close. Girl was always smart, she learned when she made a mistake. She was just always too charged up to see mistakes before her hands and feet moved toward them. Sarahi never disappointed me or any other staff at Babylon Street Elementary. She was one of those kids who kept the adults full of storytelling and shakes of the cabeza because of her—as we teachers say in our disciplinary parlance—choices. Your choices, that's what determines your life, nothing else but you and your choices. Make better choices. We alternately massage and hammer that slogan into the prefrontal cortices of our students' young, mushy brains hoping the discipline at our school will improve. It rarely does.

The truth about any American school, or minimum-security prison for that matter, is that no one pays attention to those who follow the rules, the good students, the well-behaved inmates, those who make the better choices; they do their time and graduate. On the other hand, the names of the nympho-, pyro-, and kleptomaniacs stay with you. It's the Sarahis and their upsetting choices you recall and memorialize. When everyone at the school knows a student's name, it's usually because everyone has had a turn at punishing him or ... her.

Sarahi was being raised by her maternal grandmother, who was old and overwhelmed and nearly the same size as the little girl. The grandmother was a woman whose body language and laissez fare attitude about parent-teacher conferences communicated her own truth, which was: *I already raised my own pinche kids. Why do I have to be here and do it again?* "Because your daughter is in jail and her baby daddy was deported back to Guata three years ago. That leaves you, Abuela. That leaves you responsible for Sarahi, Abuelita." That was the pretend conversation I would always have in my mind when I was trying to coax better parenting from the exhausted 70-year-old. I was too polite to actually say anything aloud like that, but in my daydreams I got all up in her face trying to convince her to do a better job of raising Sarahi, even if being a parent again wasn't exactly her choice.

The grandma often arrived late to school appointments even though she had no job and lived across the street. That often gave teachers and administrators the impression that Abuelita was fucking with us. Abuelita did what was required by the state; she would feed Sarahi and shelter her, sometimes comb her hair into a thick trenza, but getting the old woman to care about a report card or a field trip slip or back-to-school night attendance was like asking her to care about the effect of French existentialism on the postmodern novel. Sarahi and her gingerbread man were pretty much on their own. During our special-education meetings, when the staff finally got Sarahi qualified for special services, the grandmother would say: "Ya, ya se. Ella es bien inquieta, distraída, pero bien distraída," and then smile like she was describing a pretty outfit. Abuelita eventually would sign whatever permission slip we put in front of her. But we needed more than just signatures and adjectives for Sarahi. We would pepper the old woman with questions and suggestions: "Have you applied for free medical coverage? Maybe you could go to the Children's

Bureau for assistance? Does Sarahi have a routine for homework when she arrives home?" But, pobrecita, the viejita didn't know what to do except to nod at us and say, "Yes yes yes," and then explain, "But Sarahi is a very unquiet girl, very distracted, but very distracted." I knew, in reality, the routine after school was probably more like Sarahi getting called a demonia for tearing up the house and then being hit with an angry chancla now and then just to make the girl listen. Sometimes, just sometimes, though, Abuelita could coax Sarahi into sitting down long enough so that her grandmother could twist one hearty braid out of the girl's wild, thick, black, Indian hair.

That's what I was thinking when I looked at Sarahi's hair as we were waiting in the principal's office for the police. We were actually sequestered in Mr. Furman's small office. The principal was on his way back to school. I had told the secretary to call him on his cell because the situation was getting out of hand. "We need him here, call him," I insisted. The mother of the girl Sarahi had hurt had arrived, cussing blood and fire and screaming at everyone, berating the school's office secretaries. That mom was the one who called the police, yelling into the phone, crying too. Her daughter, Gigi, another one of my students, was crying in tandem and bleeding from her armpit. The Korean nurse spoke her broken Spanish in an attempt to calm the mother while trying to stop the bleeding at the same time. I sequestered myself and Sarahi in the principal's office because the mom wanted to get at Sarahi. She called her a "fuckin' dark girl-brat," which sounded much worse in Spanish. Sarahi was crying and trembling; her head of everywhere hair made her look electrocuted, engulfed by a wave of static. The hairdo was part of her costume. Our California History Festival was today. We were supposed to have an assembly explaining our class' costumes. Now that whole assembly was fucked. Sarahi was a mess. She was barefoot. Kind of half naked. Her blue and white facepaint had been melted onto her lips by her tears.

I could still hear Gigi's mom yelling into the phone, exaggerating, saying someone had "stabbed" her daughter. The mom was Panamanian. Big. A light-skinned mestiza-mulata with fair, freckled skin supported on some ancient, husky African frame. Through the closed door we could hear her boom-boom voice calling the nurse a "pinche china inútil," even though the nurse was born outside of Seoul. I was boiling because I wanted to yell out, "She's fucking Korean, not Chinese, Bitch!" But that would have made everything worse. Gigi's mom was enraged and wanted to see the girl who had made her girl bleed arrested or something. The situation had turned into a bona fide mitote. I could feel the wild chimpanzee-drama energy rising, even in me. The Korean nurse and the African-American secretary, along with the Latina secretary, couldn't calm the mother in any language. Alone, in the principal's office, I didn't know what to do or say to Sarahi. Interrogating her would have been futile. I had seen what happened. She had done it in front of me. What I really wanted to do was braid her mess of hair, but that's like asking me to crochet a blanket or whip up some chile rellenos. I'm fucking useless.

I walked over to the phone and called Mrs. Velasquez instead. She is a 50-something Puerto Rican lady who also teaches fourth grade like me. I told her to get down to the main office. I needed her help, NOW. "Send your class to the computer room," I suggested. I had sent mine to the playground while I escorted Sarahi by the arm to the office. I replayed in my mind what later would become known as "The Spearing": Sarahi standing up, aiming, then throwing her homemade spear across the classroom, right at Gigi. It happened fast but looked slow, as if emotion had warped time. All I saw was a ball of hair rising up like a black cloud from a desk and then a sad, flimsy spear shooting out from it like a thunderbolt.

When Sarahi would sit for her grandmother's hairbraiding sessions, when the girl was in the primary grades, her teachers knew that things might be getting better at home and, hopefully, by extension, also at school. Her trenza was often the barometer that measured her mind's weather. For a short lull, things would be calm when her braid was intact, but then something would happen and the cycle of bad choices and chimpanzee-mitote-drama would start up again. Inevitably, Sarahi would end up sitting in a chair in the main office or with the school nurse, streaked with tracks of sudor or tears, her skin dusted with black playground dirt. She would be dressed, out of dress code, in ripped jeans, a dirty t-shirt, and no socks, just her dingy tennis shoes. Her trenza, by recess time, would be destroyed, frazzled into a lion's mane. In kindergarten, I remember, the unraveling always started the same way. Sarahi had learned to use her long braid as a whip. When it was tight and long and black and rubberbanded, she would purposefully sit close to another student, often a boy, and turn her neck quickly, making the braid whip the kid in the face. Then she would act surprised and unknowing when the boy protested, her face twisted into a contrived "What? What happened? What?" The melodramatic acting was actually kind of funny. I sort of enjoyed it. By the next day, the carefully made braid would be obliterated.

The spear that Sarahi threw didn't really pierce Gigi. When Sarahi threw the spear, all my fourth graders ducked as if their years of dodgeball had finally paid off. Everyone in the class knew the target was Gigi. Sarahi's throw was sad and curved, and, because of that Gigi, weirdly, caught the spear with her armpit. She hadn't intended to catch it. She saw Sarahi aiming at her and clenched her body, and in that defensive clench Gigi caught the homemade spear under her right arm. The movement could've been slapstick. For a second it looked as if she'd been gored through the chest because the spear was sticking straight out. My heart dropped into the acid-puddle of my stomach. There's no preparation for something like that. The students didn't panic, however. They were silent, eerily silent. Inside the silence was the tremendous collective realization: Sarahi had just tried to kill Gigi. The physics of the assault never would have worked. The actual spear was about as sharp as a pushpin, but Sarahi's intent was as pointed and obvious as a Samurai's sword. She was pissed and wanted to fuck Gigi up. That's what really cut through everybody. Gigi screamed, and once she realized the spear hadn't attached to her she started screaming even louder, and shaking. I stood up, started shouting orders. The red line under Gigi's armpit began to dribble blood.

The scene was like fourth-grade Latino Shakespearean guerilla theater. I dismissed my students to the playground just to get them out of the way. I yelled at them to leave the classroom. I ordered some girls to take Gigi to the nurse. I grabbed Sarahi by the arm, probably way too hard, pulling her out of the doorway into the hallway. We headed down to the main office, following right behind Gigi, following the spots of blood on the linoleum leading downstairs. Gigi started dialing her phone. I have come to hate cell phones in elementary schools.

I think I know when life became darker for Sarahi, although I can't prove it. I wasn't her first-grade teacher, when her troublemaking went beyond the molestation of classroom furniture and assaults with trenza whips. In first grade Sarahi caused a little bit of a scandal at the school. A playground supervision aide—one of the Señoras, as the children called them—saw a little boy skipping around the schoolyard waving money in the air like a bon voyage handkerchief. Knowing how fights or tears can begin with even one lost dollar, she reprimanded the boy and ordered him to place the currency back in his pocket. He stopped and put it away. As he did, the supervision aide glanced at the dollar bill and noticed Benjamin Franklin's mug. She demanded that the boy come to her. The little punk ran away, of course. And, of course, she caught up with him later. This particular Señora discovered a $100 bill in the student's pocket. The little boy ratted out another student in his class, and then that little girl ratted out another little girl, and $500 later the Señora and the teacher were in the principal's office with five crying first graders, trying to complete a money-laundering investigation. The untangling of tattletales led to Sarahi. First she denied it, then she said someone else had given the money to her at the store, then she said she found the bundle of bills on the floor while walking to school with her mom. When she said that, all of the adults, who of course already knew this little girl's personal history, paused, knowing what a sad lie there was in her statement. They didn't know where to begin undermining her perjury: "Your mom is in jail, you live across the street, what store did you go to?" After some phone calls, the story emerged that an uncle from Lancaster was visiting and kept his rent money, which he was earning with temporary jobs in LA, stashed inside the sofa. Sticky-fingers Sarahi had jacked her own uncle, and neither the uncle nor the grandmother had yet learned of the thievery until the school called. So when the grandmother came to collect Sarahi and the money, Abuelita had a real worried look on her face because she had told the secretaries that the $500 was supposed to be $800. Where was the rest? Everyone shrugged. Sarahi couldn't answer for herself.

Sarahi didn't come to school for a week after that. When the school called home, Abuelita said she had a fever and a cough. When she returned to school, she returned with a neat trenza but she was quiet, too quiet, as if the gingerbread boy inside her had been eaten or at least all the candy details had. She still had her restlessness but was mute, kept to herself, her boogie was moving but quietly now like the timid movements of a puppy from a puppy mill. Something had happened that week she had the "fever and cough." Something had happened that cost the uncle $300 and cost Sarahi all the candy details of her gingerbread boy.

One thing I've come to realize as a teacher new to fourth grade is that the darkness of little girls is not respected. The thing about fourth-grade girls, particularly girls on the verge of breasts, hips, and the playland of makeup, is that their femininity possesses a dark shadow. The daring, expected restlessness of boys steals everyone's attention while young girls practice brutality on each other like they practice using high heels and eyeliner. Somewhere on the continuum of dark femininity, from cholas to mother superiors to imperial dragon ladies, there is a place for adolescent and teenage girls. Teachers and other adults aren't usually privy to this meanness. But if you sit quietly and pretend to not listen, or pause before you enter a room, you can overhear how some of the prettiest girls, the Gigis, are all knife words and razor looks with each other.

A few summers ago while at a teachers' conference in Palm Springs, I nearly fell victim to these faces of cutlery. Several attendees were waiting for a friend to get ready for a beautifully hot night out in the desert city. We were waiting by the hotel pool. The bears of the group had been raving about a leather bar they wanted us to carouse. As we drank mai tais and fluorescent margaritas, a gaggle of teenage girls exited the pool in loud splashes. The bikinis they sported were so tiny they looked like subtle rashes over the girls' new breasts and vaginas. A few of us smiled at their brazen clotheslessness. The nostalgia of being young, svelte, and attracting boys wafted toward us. They saw us staring and started calling us asshole perverts and dirty old men and shouted at us to stop looking at them. They were a wet gang of little bitches. Suddenly the situation felt like the Salem witch trails. I wanted to display my ninja-drag-queen black-belt skills in shit-talking and put the little bitches in their place before anyone overheard them. I fantasized about instantly teleporting them to Saudi Arabia to teach them a lesson. But before even saying a word, the two bears of our group started kissing each other and tweaking each other's nipples. The girls wrapped their towels around themselves and their itty bitty teeny weeny bikinis and hurriedly tiptoed away with a lesson about Palm Springs' nightlife. If I had had a long braid, I would've flicked it victoriously the way girls do when they win.

But the power of their sneers, of their caras twisting into cubisms of disgust and accusation, all the rolling eyes and upturned noses stayed with me. If I myself had never earned my black belt in drag-queen shit-talking what would I have had to protect myself with? I couldn't hit them. The situation seemed reminiscent of little white girls of the Jim Crow South who would call big black men "niggers" because the girls knew the men couldn't really do anything about it. That's the power of eye-rolling, gum-smacking girl-ness. They can be untouchably foul and they know nobody can do anything about it. That balmy Palm Springs experience prepared me better for what to expect in fourth grade than did any workshop at the teachers' conference. What I forgot was that it was not just about protecting myself, though. What about a little girl who had no parents, wore the same dirty shoes every day, moved around too much like a gingerbread boy, was dirt dark, and had wild Indian hair that couldn't stay squeezed into in a braid for more than a day?

Mrs. Velasquez knocked on the principal's door. "Open up. It's me. What's going on?" She looked concerned as she entered. I told her I'd explain everything in a bit. She looked at Sarahi and probably had already surmised that, of course, Sarahi was involved. But she was all compassion: "¿Mami, que tienes? ¿Que 'sta pasando, niña?" She reached out to touch Sarahi's shivering, exposed back.

Mrs. Velasquez had helped Sarahi fashion the backless costume and the jewelry she was wearing. Sarahi had memorized a three-minute speech for our assembly on California history that was supposed to take place this afternoon. Sarahi had dressed as Karana. Karana is the main character from Scott O'Dell's *Island of the Blue Dolphins*. It's a fictional story based on the nonfictional account of a girl who was stranded alone for 18 years on one of the small islands off the California coast. Toward the end of the novel Karana has grown to be a woman eager to escape her marooned, solitary life. She is finally about to leave the island, with the help of a priest and some sailors. She has spent years and years alone. In preparation for her departure she adorns herself with her best wardrobe, a self-made collection including a sea otter cape, a black cormorant skirt, a necklace of black stones, and black stone earrings. She marks her face as an unmarried woman the way she remembers her tribe doing long ago: blue and white clay stripes across her brown face. I loved that image of the character. Of course, the bookcovers always render Karana as some sweet, long-haired Latina hippie girl, as if she were advertising Maybelline's new mocha-colored foundation. Where's the angry, lonely, cracked-out indigenous girl of the actual novel? Well, apparently she was sitting in our principal's office waiting for the police to arrive. Mrs. Velasquez and I had probably been too good with our casting for the assembly.

Because she is a mom, Mrs. Velasquez immediately got to work cleaning up Sarahi. She has four children of her own and knew how to wet a napkin to wipe off facepaint and tears in a way that was tender and appropriate. She also knew how to place rubberbands in her mouth and grab fists full of hair to make some sense and civilization out of the mess atop Sarahi's head. She sent me out of the room to go get Sarahi's backpack upstairs so the child could change back into her regular clothes.

Before I began this academic year, I realized I had forgotten about the fourth-grade curriculum because the last time I had been through it was in fourth grade. But it focuses mainly on California history: the indigenous, the Spanish, the Mexican, and then ultimately the American rule of the land and its people.

Most teachers, like sweet Mrs. Velasquez, teach the Martha Stewart version of fourth-grade history, focusing on basket-weaving or acorn-smashing. Compared to the Aztecs, Maya, and Incas, the California Indians seemed sort of unevolved, subsisting on acorn gruel and living in sad little huts. I opted to teach the Quentin Tarantino version of *Island of the Blue Dolphins*, not all this arts-and-crafts bullshit. From that perspective, Karana is one badass motherfucking Indian girl. After jumping off a ship into the sea to be with her little left-behind brother, she burns down her abandoned village, hunts a sea elephant, kills a pack of wild dogs, and survives a tsunami. From a certain point of view, the story is like *Kill Bill* set on Catalina Island. Karana is a complicated, pissed-off island girl who deserves a more three-dimensional treatment by teachers. But most educators up and down California define Karana by what she makes—her baskets, her canoes, her skirt of black feathers. She's good curriculum because of what she produces, not because of what she feels. Elementary schools are really good at taking the edges off objects with a point.

When I got to my classroom, the mess looked like an emergency had happened. Desks and chairs were askew. Books and papers and backpacks lay everywhere. I knew Sarahi's backpack immediately because it was the only plain, black Jansport. Three of my students were in the room when I arrived. They were supposed to be outside.

"What are you doing in here?" I asked.

"We wanted the jump ropes." They had a ready answer.

"Well, you know where they're at."

"Is Sarahi getting suspended?" one of the girls asked.

"That's none of your business," I replied.

They starting rummaging through the cluttered closet to retrieve the jump ropes. One girl, Melissa, stopped, then interrupted: "Mr. Villalobos. We know why Sarahi did that to Gigi." I took a deep breath, knowing sooner or later I would have to hear 29 different versions of the story.

"Why?" I asked, expecting a long, convoluted soap opera told simultaneously by three garrulous girls. But instead they all looked at each other. Silent. Then Melissa reached into her pocket and handed me her cell phone. She pressed a button three times. There was a photo.

I was a little disoriented by the blur of the image, but studying it I realized it was obviously Sarahi's backside, her butt, or rather the bottom of her back and the top of her ass. It was obvious that it was Sarahi because you could see the edge of the cormorant skirt that Mrs. Velasquez had helped Sarahi make, that Sarahi had changed into at recess in order to get ready to be Karana for the assembly. You could also see the furry deep brownness of Sarahi's skin. The text below said: "Stay away from hairy crack! LOL!" The message was from Gigi.

Melissa stated the obvious, "She sent the picture to everybody, Mr. Villalobos."

"Why didn't you tell me sooner?" I asked angrily, but it was a stupid, adult question. There had already been a multitude of stolen kisses, sucker punches, and calculator use during math tests that had gone on without my knowledge during the year. My question now was like asking an injured mafioso why he hadn't called the FBI for help. Fourth graders have their own private California, and keep it to themselves most of the time.

When Sarahi ended up being my student again in fourth grade, she wasn't the only one. There were other children who had been my students in kindergarten. But I remembered the trouble I had with her the most, or at least I thought I remembered the trouble. She came with such a well-earned reputation that I couldn't distinguish what I had experienced myself and what I had overheard in the faculty lounge. However, by fourth grade children can hold actual conversations with a teacher, and this opens them up to becoming people. There was one moment when I actually felt love and admiration for Sarahi. Not as a child but as a person. I saw her as a person. It was with her mission project. Building a replica of a Spanish mission is practically part and parcel of the California State standards. I always wonder what other states have their students build replicas of.

The day the students carried in their miniatures and made their presentations, we all peered into their quaint versions of missions Santa Barbara and Capistrano and Obispo. There were belfries and arches made out of cardboard, sugar cubes, and lasagna noodles, and more than a few were Build-a-Mission kits sold for $29.99 at local craft stores. Then Sarahi came in with hers. It was Mission San Gabriel. Her version, however, was half burnt, and she had little priests lying prone in pools of red paint to look like blood. A figure of a lady stood amongst Indian figurines looking more like bloodthirsty Apaches than Gabrielinos. Sarahi said the diorama was based on Toypurina's 1785 attack on Mission San Gabriel.

As she made her presentation, she brought my heart into my throat because I knew nobody had helped her. Not one dollar had been given to her, not one piece of advice. In fact her grandmother was probably annoyed with all the mess her project had made in the house. The model was the product of pure intellectual curiosity, pure resiliency, nothing but the desire to complete a story I had made passing reference to in class. I had to stop myself from tearing up as she talked about Toypurina's failed, premeditated, but unactualized attack on Mission San Gabriel. Of course, only a gay Chicano studies nerd-teacher would cry over a diorama of an attack on one of the California missions. But I did. No one would understand that, so I kept the emotion to myself. I gave her a 4, of course. That's an A. Later on I pulled her aside to tell her her project was the best one, "Really Sarahi, I want you to know you did a really good job." She asked me a question, moving her feet back and forth, her gaze bouncing everywhere, unable to be still: "Mr. Villalobos, what does it mean, banish? I didn't understand on the website what banish means."

"That means they sent her away and she couldn't return to her home." Sarahi stood silently as she took in the answer. I decided to probe a little more: "Can you imagine how scared and brave Toypurina must have been to try to attack the Mission? The building was huge compared to the Gabrielino homes. It probably was the biggest structure around."

Sarahi stood quiet, then offered, "Yeah, it must have been like attacking a skyscraper." And with that she ran off to get her snack for recess without saying goodbye. She left me silent at my desk, wondering if she understood what she had just said.

By the time I came down with the backpack containing her clothes, and Melissa's cell phone, the police had arrived at the main office. A man and a woman. Gigi's mom immediately approached them. The female officer escorted her into the nurse's office. The male officer walked over to where Sarahi, Mrs. Velasquez, and I were standing. After examining Gigi and listening to the hysterical mother, the female police officer walked over, whispered something into the ear of her partner and then announced to Sarahi: "We're going to have to take you to the police station, okay? This is very serious." By then the secretaries were on the phone attempting to reach Abuelita and the principal. The police were going to take Sarahi.

Karana actually had a secret name, Won-a-pa-lei, which supposedly meant the Girl with the Long Black Hair. I don't know if author Scott O'Dell made that language up or actually researched it. But the real woman the story is based on, Maria Juana, ultimately was retrieved from her island and relocated to Santa Barbara. The eyewitnesses said Maria Juana was dressed in shag skin and her hair was matted, tangled, and dense like the hair of disturbed, homeless people. Five weeks after her arrival on the mainland, after gorging herself on fruits and vegetables she had never tasted before, Maria Juana became ill and died. She was buried somewhere at Mission Santa Barbara. No one knows where.

The police let Sarahi change into her regular clothes, which I had brought down from the classroom. Ms. Velasquez looked suddenly tired. The police didn't put handcuffs on Sarahi, but she became reluctant to move. Once the female cop reached out for her, she began crying in a way that made anyone close to her feel lonely. I felt lonely. Ms. Velasquez hugged her and was speaking Puerto Rican cariños in her ear. The secretaries, the nurse, random people who had wandered into the main office unexpectedly, stood around looking on as the police officers waited for the hug to end. It was the largest number of adults that had ever paid attention to Sarahi at one time. Her largest audience would've been at our California history assembly if she had made a different choice. But that wasn't going to happen now.

I handed the cell phone Melissa gave me to the male officer, explaining what was on it. He took it and placed it in his front pocket without a thank-you. When the female cop placed a hand on Sarahi's shoulder to end the hug, Sarahi cried out like a toddler. She was 5 years old again. The braid Ms. Velasquez's had made out of Sarahi's dark thick Indian hair made her look much younger than her 10 years. The police officers escorted her out as everyone looked on but pretended not to. They took over the matter and left us all to finish the school day.

I never saw Sarahi again. Although a Department of Social Services worker came to speak to me briefly a week after "The Spearing," she wouldn't answer any of my questions because of privacy policies surrounding "the case," as she called it. Later the school's main office staff had me fill out Sarahi's cumulative record so that they could send it off to her new location, someplace I had never heard of in the Valley.

No one ever came to claim Sarahi's left-behind possessions. Her books, her black backpack, her pencils and erasers. Nothing. They just stayed inside her cluttered desk. I didn't let anyone touch her things or sit at her desk. No student ever replaced her. By the end of the school year, Sarahi's diorama of Toypurina's 1785 attack on Mission San Gabriel sat way in the grimy corner of our classroom's highest closet like a small, ignored piece of forgotten history.

Me calientes como una plancha

The family gun had been hiding in my parents' bedroom since before my birth; it was familia before I was. Like most guns it played a salacious hide-and-seek with us children, revealing itself once in while, teasing us with surprise, naked peek-a-boos. But because we were trained to understand that it was not shared property in the same way the remote control or the forks or the Nissan Sentra were, we children deliberately chose to feel fulfilled instead by our blip-blip-blip-ing video games and colorful, plastic toys. The gun was Papi's, only.

His black Beretta, however, waited patiently for decades of discipline to erode and a childhood amnesia to weaken. Our reunion was what I received when I prayed to God, "Please, please, please help get me the fuck up out of my job." When you use cuss words to pray to God, He cusses right back. But He can't say, "God damn you!" because that would be ridiculous. Instead, He smolders villages, smites villagers, and creates the typhoons and monsoons that move the unmovable and inundate the empty.

I felt empty and unable to move every day that I sat anchored at my desk. Taking the Beretta to Babylon Street Elementary was not an accident, but by the time I chose to do so the monsoon swelling inside me whipped and ripped at my mind's flimsy flag of reason. "The cop outfit is incomplete without the gun," was my sad little pennant of logic. The double firing was what was unexpected; the gunrunning, I have to admit, had been premeditated.

When a gun fires it leaves a heat in the metal of its barrel. The heat lasts longer with more firings. When the double firing happened, the cold gun I had brought to work was hitting the linoleum floor of the school's supply room in hot, nasty clack-clack-clacks.

Minutes before the clack-clack-clacking, I was in my office, at my desk, immersed in a story on the Internet about a teenybopper white girl sailing around the world by her lonesome. She had, a day earlier, embarked safely from the Seychelles but had bobbed into the swirl of a developing storm. As the weather swallowed her boat, her radio unexpectedly cut off. Those who love her were searching with radar and heart-clogged throats for her blip-blip-blip presence on their green computer screens. Calling her un-answering satellite phone, they felt insane as they dialed and redialed and redialed.

I was just east of the Seychelles with the girl, a stowaway in the freewheeling whiteness of her circumnavigation, when Ezekiel came back into my office after having left just minutes before with little Juanito. As I looked at Ezekiel, taking in the peculiarity of him returning, I could feel the breeze of the approaching weather coming to eat the blond girl bobbing on the sea. The frightening exhilaration she must've felt measuring the clouded sky from the little prow of her little boat, surrounded by too-much ocean, I felt in my own chest, sitting in my own chair in my office. When Ezekiel stood by the door and asked me the whereabouts of my leather bracelet, I knew, with his provocation, we would end up in the supply room. That's where the stormy, hot tumult sloshing inside me could finally be divulged.

Babylon Elementary locks up its paper, scissors, and single provision of silence in a small, well-stocked supply room. Whenever Mr. Ezekiel, the teacher's aide responsible for maintaining the room, enters to pluck, say, a shrink-wrapped brick of pupil-suspension forms, two resident rats politely withdraw into their gnawed-out labyrinth within the school's walls. Mr. Ezekiel would always make a racket as he entered, hoping to scare the rats off if they hadn't already heard the key click into the keyhole. However, this time when he and I entered the supply room together, we were stealthy and quiet and smiling with nervous, wet teeth. I was a cop, he was himself.

The supply room is located kitty-corner to a little-used school exit often featured in my getaway fantasies. Sometimes when I leave to lunch, I find the piss stains and wall writings of Mara Salvatrucha gangbangers on the outside doors. Pushing through the double doors temporarily relieve my repetitious thoughts of "How do I get out of this place?"

There are, however, only three ways teachers actually leave Babylon Street Elementary: they retire, die, or have a clumsy affair with a coworker and then transfer in the frenzied double-heat of lust and shame. This was my final year at Babylon, but retirement was decades away. That left dying, falling in love, and my bad-word prayers.

Being a cop, my dad hid his firearm under his underwear in the top right drawer of my parents' dresser. In our home, he was the giant with the fee-fi-fo-fum appetite. His three brown children were Englishmen with smelly blood. The dresser that vaulted my parents' adult possessions was always unlocked, but protected from their children's fingers and stares by an enchantment: "If you so much as look at the knob to the drawer of the dresser where the gun is, I will kick your little asses and then eat you up." Papi was Cronos and had bewitched the dresser with cannibal promises. The fear of having my ass kicked and then eaten laid a strip of amnesia onto my head, allowing me to wake every day with the relief of forgetting that there was always a murder weapon available in my house. I would successfully forget, of course, until the next peek-a-boo.

Throughout all of last year, the Mrs. Greenburg-Mr. Greenberg-Ms. Choi love triangle enthralled Babylon's staff, organizing the audience of teachers into camps of loyalty, fascination, and snickering. The faculty lunch room gossip built itself up higher and higher upon the scandalous trigonometry as the year progressed. Almost everyone rooted for Mrs. Greenburg, the roly-poly wife of Mr. Greenburg. I sided with her, too, although I thought Ms. Choi had the obviously better wardrobe. Her black Gucci slingbacks were my favorites. Ms. Choi began her well-heeled home-wrecking with questions brought to Mr. Greenburg, the lead science teacher, about how to teach her second graders the water cycle. Her inquires initially justified her place at Mr. Greenburg's usually all-male lunch table. But the burgeoning couple's talk of precipitation and evaporation seemed to create more rumors than second-grade lessons.

The pair's subsequent lunches had all the women cutting looks at Ms. Choi and whispering reports to an overwhelmed Mrs. Greenburg, who, to her misfortune, had a later lunch hour and preferred Skechers tennis shoes. By the end of the school year, the entire staff had exhausted themselves with vicarious angst and tension to the point where even those loyal to Mrs. Greenburg were relieved that all the protagonists volunteered to transfer from Babylon.

My dad never fetish-ized his gun. It was simply part and parcel to his uniform, as necessary as his black boots, his black rechargeable flashlight, a sweat-stained bullet-resistant vest, and a badge crowned by a silver California grizzly. Every two weeks or so, he would clean his gun, shine his boots, and flay his starched uniforms, fresh from the cleaners, of their plastic covering. His Sunday-night preparation ritual was held in our living room, and if I happened to pass by, I snuck a peek at the gun's naked blackness. But I tried to ignore it because I was a good, bewitched amnesiac of a child.

On dark Monday mornings, from my bed, I could smell coffee brewing and hear rustlings as Papi dressed for work with the swift, meticulous efficiency of an ex-Marine. The gun's "bye-bye" would be muffled as it was placed in its black leather holster. My amnesia would recommence once I heard the door close.

I didn't realize in September of the new school year that this would be my final year at Babylon Street Elementary. I had no immediate plan to leave the salary, pension, and vacation time, despite my growing loathing for the job. But the school's mascots of Lust and Death hung around, sleepy and bored by the departure of the Greenbergs, the Gucci-ed Ms. Choi, and the long-departed, before-my-time teachers who had left Babylon because their cancers mutilated them beyond use, their diabetes had hobbled them, and, one in particular case, heart disease had given Mrs. Kulani an opportunity to finally rest in peace and will her daughter the monetary benefits of 30 years of teaching third grade.

My cussing and praying began when the village of Babylon Street Elementary, kids, parents, and teacher-folk, began their tattletelling and shunning and selecting of stones for my stoning. What began as petty grievances played out like rounds of rock-paper-scissors that quickly escalated into an honor killing. One day, alone, after a week of tumult from having removed Juanito's shoes, rummaged through Esdras' backpack, and towed one Mercedes, I prayed to God, "Please, please, please get me the fuck up out of my job."

When I found my dad's old uniforms boxed away in the garage, I thought how awesome it was that my ass and legs were the same size as his ass and legs had been when he last wore those pants. As I held them up to me, measuring the length, the strip of amnesia applied during my obedient boyhood lifted, and the Beretta reappeared in my head. I hadn't seen it in years. I doubted it was in the garage. It probably still lay under Papi's underwear on the male side of my parents' hermaphroditic dresser.

At the bottom of the box of uniforms, I then spotted a belt. I picked up the black police belt, as thick and satisfying as a whip, braided in the middle like a leather trenza, and held it to my nose. I breathed deeply, savoring the irrepressible good stink of cop leather.

I once wore my leather cock ring to work. Accidentally, of course. I had gone out on a Tuesday night to Rimjob in Silverlake to celebrate George's 33rd birthday. I had been teasing my best friend that this was his Jesus

Christ birthday, the year to symbolically die and be reborn. "Fuckyoubitch," George insisted, "I'm Buddhist, like Thich Nhat Hanh."

"What the fuck's that?" I asked.

"Just get your ass ready quick-like. We have to be there before 10. I'm not standing in no line just because you take too long trying to look cute. It don't ever work." He hung up with a stupid cackle.

Esdras Villacencio dreaded coming to school because of what his mom might do while he was in class. Like clockwork, every day, 18 minutes after being dropped off by his mother, the third grader's mouth would swell into plump pucheros and he would begin to whimper, then sob, then wail until he had to be led out into the hallway by an exasperated teacher. Ms. Glassman, the school psychologist, would be called for assistance. She would coax him to her office and display her colorful, plastic toys and ask him questions about his feelings. But he would cry unceasingly because there was an ocean trapped inside him that could only leave through two puny pinholes near his eyes. The pain of too much something inside a body so little hurt to the point where he couldn't even talk. He was choked by a visceral, pulsing ocean with an oversupply of water. Ms. Glassman eventually would relent and call his mom to return to pick up her inundated child. Ms. Glassman would say to the Spanish-speaking mother, "He's too old to be acting like this." The relief of seeing his mom receded the ocean until 18 minutes into the next school day, when the water cycle inside Esdras would begin all over again.

I didn't own black Gucci slingbacks like Ms. Choi, but my black leather cock ring, which I wore as a bracelet, helped me work it out the way women work gold bangles or cleavage. When I met George at the bar, he noticed the cock ring on my left wrist right away. "Either your wrist is too small or maybe we should be more than friends," he joked. We drank and danced. We toasted beer bottles, I paid for birthday shots of tequila, and we provided Latino-boy strippers with their rent money in folded singles. George kept extending the schoolnight with peals of "But it's my birthday!" He had us stay until the bar closed, then we ran next door to chow down nightcap tacos at a turquoise taqueria. The sky faded into the color of a taqueria as I drove home with my windows rolled down, hoping the wind could keep me from falling asleep and dying in a sunrise car wreck.

Every morning after sunrise, Chelo would walk her son Juanito to kindergarten, but he always skipped ahead of her as her chanclas scratched out a huevona "ch-ch-ch-ch" on the sidewalk behind him. The kindergartner would pick up a stick and strike saplings and litter and roses-entwined fences. Sometimes, without looking at his mother, he would suddenly ask for the toy, the dollar, the candy, the chips with limón and chile he had been promised. Lately, he had upped the ante, "¿Mami, cuando va a venir Papi?"

His young mother would strike back immediately: "¡Ya te dije, niño! No sé. No sé. ¡Como chingas tú!" Juanito would shut his mouth and return to smashing roses to smithereens with his branch, leading his mom who was walking him to school.

I arrived at work with an ache around my eyes. I had been home only to brush my teeth. No one said anything about my disheveled appearance. Except Ezekiel, or Mr. E., as the kids called him. Twenty years old, a student at the local community college, he worked part-time at Babylon. He spotted me in the main office. I was serving myself another cup of coffee borrowed from the secretaries' pot. "I like your bracelet, Mr.," he said. He always called me "Mr." He never used my last name, nor my first.

I looked at my wrist and felt the flush of caffeinated shame. I just barely nodded and fled the office as if I had somewhere else to be. I don't think he meant to embarrass me. Regardless, I snapped the cock ring off my wrist and stuffed it into my pocket. "George is such asshole," I said to myself as I tried to gerrymander my blame to my Buddhist best friend. "Bitter, you're just bitter, Bitch," I knew he would say in his defense.

This new school year, after a decade in the classroom, I left teaching and took an administrative position because George was right.

God half-smote Papi. He was in the hospital with a heart clogged with decades of carne asada sebo, too much worry, and 30 years of carrying a gun and just almost using it, but never really using it, except if you count the time he killed a rabid dog. The doctor had explained the disease and surgery to us: a valve-atrial something-or-other with a much-needed stent. I was at the hospital every day after work, waiting for the smiting to wear off. My mother, however, would send me back to The House to retrieve cash, clothes, documents, and pillows that smelled like us.

I closed the garage and placed the box of my father's uniforms in my car. Having remembered the gun, I received the opportunity to test the potency of an old fee-fi-fo-fum force field while the cannibal slept in a hospital bed.

My parents' house was spooky; their bedroom had become a cold, zoological diorama. It felt like an empty polar bear habitat after all the polar bears of the world had been hunted or drowned. The spark and heat of their 1970s bedroom had cooled. When their bodies and organs were young, they infused the house, the furniture, the dishes and spoons, the iron, the toaster, the oven, and the walls with the hot vibrancy of young marriage. All that electricity seemed greatly diminished now. All the yelling, lovemaking, fisticuffs and slaps, the money conundrums, clumsy spankings, routine work mornings, the blaring records of people only a few years out of their teens, the cooking smells of rice in oil and water with tomatoes and onions, the brewing of coffee, bear hugs and kitten cariños, and the careful cleaning of a work firearm had once pushed daily life along an edge where a fit of laughter, an argument, a game, a feast, a belt-whipping, or a mother dancing with her children while sweeping the floor could erupt spontaneously and jumble the house at any moment. As a kid, I never knew what the household would offer: a knife could be used to tighten a screw, a belt to constrict the behavior of the children, lemons were medication, the dresser an armory.

I easily punctured through the weakened force field of the drawer. I slipped my hand under my dad's underwear. The gun was there, as faithful as buried pirate treasure. I picked it up and touched it for the first time ever. It was heavy but made for hands. My hungry right hand felt satiated. "Finally," the floorboards creaked. My heart felt gaping, open to the scientific delight of holding exceptional matter, the likes of moon rocks, ancient jewelry, anthrax in a Petri dish, a new species of beetle. The gun didn't need batteries or gasoline or to be charged up or plugged in. It was ready. It extended my hand into powerful android capability, a futuristic, robotic talon like the television's remote. All the gun needed was intention and aim ... and bullets, of course. I didn't know how to open it. How do you check to see if a gun has bullets? You have to shoot it, to be sure, I thought.

When the school psychologist, Ms. Glassman, called for assistance Friday morning, I ran to her office, the keys to all of the school's doors slapping against my thigh. Her desk had been pushed onto its side and two chairs overturned. File folders and paper carpeted the floor in a flat bouquet of fluorescent colors. Eight-year-old Esdras was red faced, hollering as if he had just been birthed, panting for his mom. "Exorcism?" I asked Ms. Glassman.

She smiled, despite this being her third week dealing with Esdras and his "birinches," as his mother kept trying to call the over-the-top rampages. The mother's euphemisms left the psychologist exasperated: "This is it! This is it! I'm through with this, Mr. Villalobos. We need to call the hospital! This is beyond what I should be dealing with." She drooped, discouraged by her laptop computer splayed on the floor.

"Let's do it," I encouraged her. "The family has been adequately notified that we would call the hospital if he got too violent," I added in administration-speak, giving Ms. Glassman something she could quote for the eventual report she would have to write.

"The hospital's number is on my phone," Ms. Glassman pointed to the petite Louis Vuitton trapped behind Esdras, "in my purse." He stood, still erupting like a broken fountain of screams, spurting out soggy bellows of: "Mami! Mami! Mami!"

"I'll get it," I said determinedly, referring to Ms. Glassman's little brown Louis.

Esdras must've thought I was charging at him, because as I moved forward, he grabbed a toy robot Ms. Glassman kept to entertain the children she worked with. He grabbed it and flung it as if he were a gladiator defending his life. I threw up my hands, but it flew between them and hit my face. The robot had an ear-like appendage that sliced my lip open. My lip burst into holy stigmata. Ms. Glassman sucked in a gulp of surprised air. I shouted a bloody, "What the fuck?!" I wanted, I really, really wanted to hit him, grab him, hold Esdras in the air until he gave up the psychosis of his rampage. He ran like a rodent into another corner of Ms. Glassman's overturned office, still screaming for his mother.

As I held my hand to my mouth, drooling blood, Ms. Glassman, in a pencil skirt and heels, bounded over the chairs and the kaleidoscopic pattern of scattered neon papers to retrieve her fancy handbag. She dialed as I sought out a dislocated tissue box. Thirty minutes later, Esdras was strapped onto a gurney and loaded into an ambulance on his way to 72 hours of observation, Ms. Glassman was writing an incident report, and I was bleeding into the last gauze pad the school nurse had in her infirmary. I went through her entire box of gauze before the slice in my lip quieted itself with the miracle of coagulation. "You need more gauze," I told Nurse Kwan.

The supply room at Babylon Elementary is a teachers' Candyland, a Candyland forested by shelves of school supplies whose metal branches offer crops of pencils and markers and paintbrushes in a perpetual Giving Tree harvest. It is the vault that stores our end-time supply of masking tape.

Only three people had the key to Candyland: Principal Furman, Ezekiel, and me. Every Friday, Mr. E. would leave kindergarten to go fill teachers' wish lists for more paint, more sponges, more crepe paper and pipe cleaners to craft the bouquets of celebratory, fake flowers needed to adorn a school over the course of a year.

I offered to retrieve boxes of gauze for Nurse Kwan, but I did so because I wanted to be alone. Candyland also supplied a cave, a chapel, a provision of silence. It was dimly lit by 1950s light fixtures and possessed a stillness older than the school—a quiet extraordinary on a campus inhabited by 900 children. The pain on my mouth kept me pissed. I let myself into the supply room and paced in residue anger up and down the cul de sacs of piled-up school supplies. I licked the slice of metallic heat on my lip obsessively. Esdras was a little shit. An open box of extra-large paperclips offered itself. I selected one at a time and twisted the flat spiral of each body into a model of crooked thoughts. I stood there, sculpting the paperclips into "I hate being here, I hate being here, I hate being here" sculptures and then into crooked rebuttals of, "but I can't afford to leave, but I can't afford to leave, but I can't afford to leave."

Mr. Ezekiel opened the door. I pretended I was looking for masking tape. He said, "Hey, Mr."

"Where's the gauze? Where do you keep the nurse's supplies?" I asked.

He walked over to a high shelf and pointed. I was taller than he was, so I reached over him and grabbed three boxes myself. I noticed that his arm hair was a mix of light brown with thin strands of gold, and he wore a trendy watch with a thick black leather band. Three boxes in hand, I slipped past him and out the door, forgetting to say thank you. The mess of my crooked thought-sculptures lay on the floor.

I lied. I had touched the gun before. Or it had touched me. Papi had taken me to a dental appointment when I was 5. After the visit, stunned by the trauma of novocaine and three fillings, I sat in the front seat of the car, my cheeks numb and drool stringing from my unfeeling lips. As we were leaving the parking lot, a car pulled out in front of us. My father had to brake hard. I jerked forward. He honked, and tossed a "What the fuck?" out the window. The other car stopped, and two cholos sprang out like a double-headed, ghetto jack-in-the-box. Their car trapped ours in the driveway. They first checked to see if their Oldsmobile Cutlass Supreme was injured. I don't think they saw me initially, because my head didn't go over the dashboard too much. They probably thought my dad was alone.

I could see the pelones glance at their bumper and then turn the lasers of their stares toward my dad. Their eyes were hateful but pretty. They extended their arms and turned their palms upward like a priest would do before turning Jesus into a cookie. They chucked their chins in that "What the fuck?" reciprocal kind of questioning. Pleito, they were transubstantiating pleito. My dad reached over to open the glove compartment in front of me. He grabbed his Beretta. I had forgotten my dad owned a gun. But he fumbled as he went for it. The gun dropped onto my thigh. He recovered it quickly, expertly, placing it in his lap. Seeing that, and maybe even noticing me, a drooling, dumbstruck kid, the cholos walked back to their car backwards, taking their time. They drove off in a loud cloud of muffler racket. I remembered the quick, heavy pat of the cold gun on my little thigh, and the handsomeness of the cholos. They had calligraphy on their bodies, and their bald heads made their pupils blaze prominently, without the distraction of a head of hair. My father returned the gun to the glove compartment. It was then that I noticed my babas pooling in the folds of my shirt, as if the small, burgeoning weather inside me had sprung a leak.

When Mr. Ezekiel came for me on Monday, I thought he was going to mention the paperclip mess I had made in the supply room. Instead, there was problem. "Mr., Ms. Willis is having trouble with Juanito. And the principal is in a meeting."

As we walked to Ms. Willis' classroom, he apprised me that Juanito had kicked two girls, again. We had already benched him, given him quiet time, had a conference with his young mom, Chelo, who offered a limp: "No sé que puedo hacer. Él no me hace caso a mi." She was baby-daddy-less and useless, always promising Juanito cheap toys and warm corn on a stick if he would behave at school. But he never did.

Before we walked in, I paused at the door of the kindergarten classroom, looking at Mr. E. He was shorter than I. His face had the variegated glisten of pirate's treasure—brown wood, yellow and blond highlights, specks of gold, red-haired slivers in his soft mustache, gems of hazel green eyes, pink lips, white teeth, a mestizo spray of skin tones. He was wearing the small tribal ear plugs guys like these days. He made my 35 seem like the horizon of his 20. There was silence as he looked at me expectantly, waiting. I turned my smile at Mr. E. into a scowl and opened the door.

The disciplinarian's skit had begun. "I'm sorry, Ms. Willis. I hate to interrupt everyone's learning, but I hear there is a problem with kicking in this class?"

Like any teacher, Ms. Willis picked up her side of the improvisation quickly. "Yes. Yes, Mr. Villalobos. We have someone in here who has a problem keeping his feet to himself." The audience of children was dead silent; suddenly, the lesson had changed from counting apples in a drawn tree to a surprise trial. The accusation and evidence were named simultaneously. "Sharon, can you show Mr. Villalobos your leg?" Ms. Willis continued.

A little girl stood up, gravely walked over to me and modeled a skinny brown leg. It had a white-person Band-Aid on it. But the bandage didn't cover the long cut or blossoming bruise. "What happened?" I asked her.

Before she could answer, a tattletale shouted out, "Juanito kicked her."

That outburst let another kid offer: "Yeah. He did. I seen him."

I could see on the periphery of the class rug Juanito drooping and pretending to be interested in some carpet lint. Ms. Willis interrupted: "Mr. Villalobos, I don't know what to do. This has been going on for the past three weeks. He doesn't listen to me. He's hurt many...."

I interrupted her testimony. "Juanito, come here." Silence. Stillness. A Long Pause. "Juanito. Come. Here." I repeated and then pointed to the square of linoleum at my feet. Juanito stood up and walked to me. I picked him up and sat him on one of the low tables. He seemed a little surprised by the uplift. Then, in two swift scoops, I took his shoes from him. "If you are going to be kicking your classmates, I am going to take your shoes so you won't hurt anybody else. You don't learn. You keep using your shoes as weapons." I dramatically tucked his small, worn out, too-cute tennis shoes under my arm. As he sat on the table, lowering his head, his dirty blue-and-white stripped socks hung like sooty stockings; an audience of his teacher and peers sat captivated. Finally, despite himself, the waterworks broke open. His dark, intense stare was blacker but shinier because of his tears. His eyes looked like quivering obsidian marbles.

"Do you understand?" I questioned softly, lowering my face toward his. He nodded in defeat.

I gave him back his shoes to put back on himself. As I walked out, without a word to anybody, I met Mr. E.'s eyes and felt my mouth gush with babas.

On Wednesdays, the city of Los Angeles cleans Babylon's neighborhood streets, creating swaths of no-parking zones and lots of pleito. Dirtied by chancla-ed mama hens shuffling their pollitos to school in the morning and Mara Salvatrucha gang members pissing in the crevices at night, the curbs are emptied for their municipal scrubbing. This transforms the school's parking lot into a metallic quilt of Mercedes, Prii, trucks and minivans squeezed together the way people squeeze into subways in cities where people take subways to work. Teachers, determined to keep their property close by, select precarious edges and obnoxious positions in order to park their vehicles within the gated campus.

On this Wednesday, a district semi arrived to deliver pallets of copy paper and one unordered package of pleito. The semi's big ass backed onto the driveway ramp of the parking lot, which also was occupied, near the bottom, by 15 industrial-sized trash bins. There were teachers' cars squeezed by each wall and two parked perpendicularly in front of the trash bins. I had sent memoranda and notices on rose-pink paper imploring teachers that they shouldn't, couldn't park like that. Once the semi backed in, the driver realized he had become part of a brainteaser of school infrastructure.

I came out to help the truck driver extricate himself from the driveway without denting schoolteacher vehicles. But after several attempts and head scratches, frustrated by the amount of time the conundrum was eating up and the history of my ignored rose-colored memoranda, I decided to open that package of pleito. The tow truck arrived minutes after my call.

Thursday morning, Ms. Glassman called me to her office offering an update: "Esdras' mother is coming to pick up his things. She is threatening to transfer Esdras to another school before I can finish any report. She won't agree to a formal assessment. His records show he has already been enrolled in two other schools this year. She keeps moving him from school to school."

Ms. Glassman had uprighted her office, although evidence of Esdras' rampages were still evident in the nicks and scratches on her furniture. "She's hiding something," I told Ms. Glassman.

"I know," she responded, "I just want someone to be here with me when she arrives. She can be a little intimidating. Can you stay?"

I moved toward an occupied chair.

Esdras' jacket, textbooks, lunch bag, and backpack were in the corner of her office, set aside since the day he had been strapped into a gurney and wheeled away in an ambulance. I picked up Esdras' backpack to move it off the chair. It felt heavy. Too heavy for third grade. "What's in here?" I asked as I began to open it. The backpack held a large porcelain figurine, some lipsticks, a hairbrush with hair tangled in the bristles, an empty perfume bottle, crumbled coupons, a credit card, earrings, and a dirty, folded up note. As I unfolded the note, Ms. Glassman said I probably shouldn't be doing that, but it was too late, the curlicues of the Spanish brought me in word by word:

Pienso en ti cada minuto, cada segundo. Me estoy volviendo loca, pero bien loca sin ti. Cuando estamos juntos me calientes como una plancha, niño. ¿Cuando podemos dormir juntos otra vez? ¿Dónde nos podemos encontrar?

I was smiling, reading the words in a gossipy whisper as Ms. Glassman kept asking, "What? What? What does that mean?"

Esdras' mother stepped into the doorway and saw the audience of her stolen things sitting with the school psychologist and everyone, everything listening to me read her love letter aloud. She walked up to me, eyes wide in instant recognition, and snatched the note, swept her possessions back into her son's backpack, and walked out the door barely contained. Ms. Glassman looked at me as if I were dented furniture.

Thursday's faculty meeting was a rumble. The teachers had carefully selected their stones for the stoning. One Mercedes had been towed and 10 teachers received $60 parking tickets. I remained unapologetic. The teachers were livid. They quoted from the contract and from conversations with the union and the school police and the office of staff relations. They had done their research and they Knew Their Rights. When I threw out, "But do you know your responsibilities?" the box of pleito had been opened and distributed.

There was the gaggle of snide, old bachelors whose greatest teaching talent was out-sassing fifth graders. They were Mr. Greenburg's former lunch crew. They took the lead at the meeting. They took turns shouting about being disrespected and underappreciated and how now there was a loss of trust on a campus that once had been a big, happy family. I rolled my eyes like a fifth-grade girl.

"Just don't park where you're not supposed to," I interrupted their excuses. But they all gnashed their terrible teeth and rolled their terrible eyes and showed their terrible claws.

"A happy teacher is a good teacher!" shouted Mr. Ellis, who spends his summers in third-world countries where there is great surfing and inexpensive dark women. "And no one is happy, Mr. Villalobos. That's because of you!".

"Then maybe you need your Thai girl prostitute fix before summer, Mr. Ellis, so your teaching can improve," I rebutted. There was a loud, collective moan of touché. Some of the teachers smiled angry smiles. The weaker ones gathered their sensible lunch bags and empty Tupperware containers, snatched their backpacks and purses, and fled out of the lounge. The snide and red-faced spoke up again, all at once, Principal Furman's control of the meeting having been lost 20 minutes before. The meeting devolved into that moment when one big story gets broken up into a hundred different personal versions, all told simultaneously. I earned two things from the faculty at the meeting, the nickname "District Rent-a-Cop" and the silent treatment.

Ms. Glassman filled me in the next day: "I spoke with the assistant principal from Esdras' last school. It turns out that Mom left him and Dad to go live with another dad from the same school, but then four months later she returned home. Or that's the school's gossip. No one can get the mom or the family to talk about anything. When the subject is broached and counseling offered, the mom changes schools. But Esdras keeps acting up at each school site."

"... because he's not sure if she will actually return to pick him up," I surmised.

"Exactly." Ms. Glassman said.

"That's fucked-up," I responded. Ms. Glassman shrugged, and then warned, "I hear she's gone to the District about you."

"Where do I go to complain about her?" I asked.

It was Mr. Ezekiel who warned me that Juanito's mother had come to make me apologize. Juanito had told her how I took his shoes from him. When she arrived at the main office, Chelo wore skinny jeans that molded her into the silhouette of a Los Angeles fertility goddess. Her hoop earrings made her look fiercely tribal, as did her long, drawn-in eyebrows. She looked Meso-American gangsta. When she came to visit Principal Furman to demand that I apologize to her and her son and to rhetorically ask who did I think I was, she obviously had spent some time in front of the mirror applying colors to her face and to her complaint.

Juanito's dad had left, maybe six months ago, maybe three. She was alone and young and inept at parenting but she Knew Her Rights. I heard her say that over and over to Mr. Furman as I pretended to look for something in the main office so that I could remain within earshot.

It was later that day that I found the letter in my staff mailbox advising me that I had the right to seek representation. Mr. Furman had agreed with Chelo, in part. He had decided that the removal of footwear could be considered corporal punishment and that, as he sought administrative process, I had a right to seek union representation.

Esdras' mother filed an illegal search complaint. I received an email notification from the District that an investigation would commence and that my direct supervisor had been notified. The stress of losing rounds of rock-paper-scissors began to hurt. Everything that I picked, the village picked one better: their rights on paper, a sharper scissor point, and bigger, bigger stones to throw. Every little boy knows that the only winnable option in a final round of rock-paper-scissors is turning your fingers into a gun.

Halloween was George's idea. Dressing up as a traffic cop would piss everyone off without having to say a word, he argued. "I could use my dad's old uniforms," I suggested as he smiled, seeing that I was game. He lent me some reflective aviator sunglasses not only because they went with the dress-up, but also, he said, because I could look at people without them seeing my eyes.

Using the gun was my own idea. The leather belt came with a leather holster. I filled the holster with the gun I had swiped from my parents' dresser. When I slipped the Beretta into the holster, the weight felt like extra appendage of vigilance and vigor.

When the teachers encountered me in my costume Halloween morning, they remained dedicated to their vow of silence. I don't think anyone noticed the gun in the holster. Or if they did, maybe they thought it was fake, like a swashbuckler's plastic sword. At one point that afternoon, I found myself alone in the hallway with two of the old bachelors. One took the opportunity to shout to another across the hallway, "Hey man, who's your least favorite member of the Village People?"

"What would George say? What would George say?" I asked myself, but by then too much time had passed and I'd lost my opportunity and nerve. The hallway was empty. I walked into my office and sat at my desk feeling empty and unable to move.

I began opening windows into other worlds on my computer, searching for people who had worse problems than me—a mob of poor, sexually repressed Arab men railing at something bigger than them, a drugged-up starlet about to lose her last shred of dignity, a lusty politician who liked money and pussy too much, and a little white girl lost while sailing around the world by herself. She had just embarked off the Seychelles.

Someone knocked on my office door. "Come in."

Ezekiel escorted Juanito into my office. Juanito walked in sad but looking like the cutest flaco-troublemaker the neighborhood could conjure. He was wearing a backpack that was nearly as big as he was. Mr. Furman had forbidden me to deal with him any longer, but he had not informed Ms. Willis about this.

Juanito knew my office meant trouble. He didn't look at me as they entered. Ezekiel, on the other hand, grinned as soon as he saw me all copped up. "La chota," he grinned, offering an approving chuckle. Juanito dragged himself over to my desk, and Ezekiel turned him around by the shoulder as if he were turning a giant key. Ezekiel pointed a nodding finger at the backpack.

Knowing better, I said, "Open your backpack." As he zipped it open, Juanito's crumpled-up army costume that he was to wear later popped out. He removed it, and beneath the fatigues lay the rainbow cache of his prized gun collection—green water pistol, yellow cap gun, gold cowboy gun, black SWAT gun, a plastic, silver-plated six shooter. Juanito had gathered all the firearms he had ever owned, all the guns Chelo or his long-gone dad had promised to buy him and then did, and he had packed them into his backpack and brought them to school, knowing they were contraband.

"He pointed one at Ms. Willis' head," Ezekiel reported, "She wants him suspended. She won't take him back into her classroom."

"They're not real," I said. Ezekiel shrugged.

"Only Principal Furman can suspend. I am not supposed to deal with Juanito anymore, anyway. Have him sit in the main office until the principal is available."

I kept the backpack of guns. But as Ezekiel led him away, Juanito stopped and spoke up in his brand of Spanglish, "Son mis guns." If I couldn't take away his shoes, what made me think I could take away his guns? Chelo had informed her son of his Rights.

Without standing up, I grabbed the backpack and threw it at his feet. We all heard the bag clack and slide on the floor. Juanito picked up his property and turned away. Ezekiel took him to the principal's office to wait for Principal Furman. I went on to read about the teenybopper white girl sailor sailing away from the Seychelles as if she were Ferdinand Magellan.

Ezekiel returned, this time by himself. "I like your outfit, Mr."

I sat at my desk, my eyes hidden behind sunglasses, tall cumulus clouds of rage accumulated over me, over the village of Babylon, placing us in shade. In the distance, in the doorway, an island with the iridescent glow of un-buried pirate treasure, a face colorful and cute, so beautiful you wanted to be mean to it, to smash it with lust.

"How come you're not wearing your bracelet?" Ezekiel asked.

The encounter was a stockroom-cop-daddy-Latino-on-Latino-boy mash-up of the very best XXX-rated smut true life can offer.

By the time I locked the supply room door and placed boxes up against it as a weak barricade, Ezekiel had slid his pants down and was stroking himself with an immature urgency. A young centaur in heat, is what I thought of him, so beautifully hairy it seemed the pelitos on his legs were curls of hot gold radiating off his skin. Equine, his lower body was equine and spectacular. Wowed by his Fahrenheit, there was no hesitation from me. The gape of my heart opened up by the Beretta had widened, and Ezekiel sunk into that space. I felt the berserk pleasure of smashing roses to smithereens. I immediately brought myself to him as he undid my uniform's silver buttons and zippers. I could smell hot, chewed-up spearmint breath from him. Our kissing was scratchy and forceful and full of crushed yerba buena. The inside of his mouth tasted like warm, fleshy tea.

I turned him around like a giant key and squatted. I opened up his ass and spit into him. My cop hat titled back as my tongue lashed forward. He smelled like a boy made of overripe papaya. He tasted like raw wolf. He protruded and swelled. He couldn't help but let out creaks of wanting.

I stood up and let my slobber fall onto myself and his backside, my babas cascading down as if my cheeks had no feeling. I pushed into him. The back of his head smelled like pepper and sudor. I was hot as an oven, an iron, a dryer, a toaster in a 1970s kitchen used by a young couple who sometimes hit each other when they fought and who bit when they made love.

"Hurry," Ezekiel said. I pushed hard and fast, spitting onto us again until our skin began to feel like used masking tape. I nestled my nose and lips into the shapely strip of cranium and cartilage behind his right ear, the place where a strip of amnesia might settle, allowing a person to bury thoughts of murder in a vault of forgetfulness. His buzz-cut haircut scoured the bridge of my nose, crunched my eyebrows, brushed my forehead into pinkness. His lower back hit my stomach in hungry, violent pulses. As I reached around his torso and slipped my hands under his shirt, I felt the moist, plush cataract of hair cascading from his belly button. His erection satiated my left hand.

As we jerked together, I did math. I subtracted our two leaping hearts from the thousand barely beating ones warehoused in a rat maze of classrooms surrounding us. The overwhelming refreshment of wildness that rose up inside me satisfied the pleasure of making cuss words incarnate. I felt the dark, surprised enticement adolescents feel when they find doodles of dicks and ass in their used science textbooks, schematics of how electricity works accompanied by hieroglyphics of fucking. Over our grunts we heard a classroom of chairs suddenly scrape against the hardwood floor above us. It sounded like the building groaned, "Finally." Students on the floor above us had just stood up in unison, as if their chairs had become too hot to stay seated in. As Ms. Choi's second graders had learned, heat rises and relieves the oceans of a surplus of water.

Our movement made a loose screw on the shelf we leaned upon

rhythmically click. That was syncopated by Ezekiel's breaths, which left him in short pulses. I was pushing hard, moving in the brusque way men dig holes, chop wood, steer boats in storms. Soon my police cap tumbled off my head and dropped onto the floor. My pants continued a slow slide to my ankles until the metal buckle of the leather belt and the butt of the gun, Papi's gun, the Beretta, still muzzled in the holster, started to hit the linoleum, joining the loose screw and short breaths in a beat. The clack-clack-clack-clack-clack of the symphony made the experience sound like the world's smallest earthquake, like we two together were trying to make Los Angeles shake. Our atmosphere, our humid weather of heavy breathing, the bursts of monsoon coming up out of me closed in around us so tightly that when I bit Ezekiel's small tribal ear plug, neither of us heard the sound of Principal Furman's key clicking into the keyhole or the soft scratch of a useless barricade of boxes sliding against the linoleum floor.

Principal Furman's double firing opened up a fourth way to leave Babylon Street Elementary. When you use cuss words to pray to God, He cusses right back.

Los Angeles Kindergarten Teacher's Sonnet

No one ever talked right in my house
and it hurts to go outside still.
Picked up the standard like a book louse
between pages speaking the real
-speak, authentic-speak, true
-words enounced correctly,
passed down by wordsmiths who
willed over words like jewelry.
I burly get thru my students' unease,
they too in a language dilemma,
when I say, "Take one step back, please!"
they just stare, standing, Emma
confused, until my home language returns
and I say "Move backer!" and they do learns.

The Night There Was a Blackout in a Los Angeles Neighborhood as Told to a Kindergarten Teacher by His Student
—as recorded by Richard Villegas Jr.

Tomorrow, I going
My house y las luces
Estaban 'pagadas.
Y el manager
Les apagó
Las luces.
For I was scary.
My mom put the canders.
Mi mama ponó canders.
Solo tres.
Después, no se si la tele
Se aprendió.

The Final Poem

I lost,
regretfully and unintentionally,
the silver-and-gold plated watch you gave me.
It might pop up in some dusty corner when I eventually move or vacuum,
or it might not.
Now I just ask others for the time.
My old address book finally tore away from its cover.
I got a newer, nicer one for my birthday.
As I rewrote the numbers,
I left those I no longer use
out.
Your old addresses, your old apartment's, your mother's, your cell.
The lotions and candles and perfumes we exchanged were all used up
the summer after you left.

The cute stuffed animals given made my students smile when they won
them away from me for knowing their alphabet or counting backwards
from ten to zero.

You don't owe me anything, not an apology, not a realization, not an epiphany.
We're even and settled over a year later.
All accounts are balanced, even if you don't know over what.
This poem is not even for you.
It's for me and my peace of mind.
It's my emotional Post-It note.
This is a final poem of forgiveness.
It's the expression
of my belief
as a writer
that what I write,
is.

Banda Maquina and the Dancing Tranny Double Sonnet

Tempo wrings its men of a poomb-poomb polka,
a poomb-poomb-ing, poomb-poomb-ing bota sway.
Amidst close-dancing men the drunk tranny loca
shouts a deep-voiced, "¡No me toques, güey!"
She's enthused and ludicrous, alone and baritone
like the thump from the lusty-throated tuba.
The nose-voiced lead pulls a song into a groan
as Banda Maquina's clarinets blow burbujas de scuba.
The Machine Band inhales a pool of stale, humdrum air
then pumps out circus, sexy, badass, narco-vibrations
that extract my heartbeat, placing it out there
amongst bigotes, gorras, and a history of cantante assassinations.
Happy bloodsoaked music swells. "¡Ay, me encanta la banda!"
she yells, winks, bumps, then mumbles, "Hola. Soy, soy, soy Amanda."

Banda Maquina bends breathing breath
into excellent brass whimpers and squeals.
The Mexica furnished warrior hearts beating death,
Hernán added caballos, castellano, catastrophe, and wheels,
Germans provided the polka base and Africa, the ostrich belt.
U.S. coca-mota hunger crowned the nation with traffickers
as banda had three, four, five cultures together smelt
serenades to accompany bailes, beheadings, and massacres.
Amanda, cabrona, sends out late, not-so-subliminal calls.
"Tócame, tócame," she asks a silver-toothed leftovers
standing to final songs that thrill and bleed like brawls,
hoping to dislodge just one, just one of the good-morning-glory wallflowers.
I swallow back my heartbeat, calm after the exuberance of a horn heaven—
loving the soundtrack of wounded countries and their wailing vaquero men.

Los Angeles Times, Test Scores, and Other Caca

I looooooove to see teachers get riled up. When a faculty made up of old white women, Jews and Asians, some gays, and young Latinas gets angry, it's like watching the beginning of a really bad joke turn into a revolution. The walls of the faculty lounge seem to vibrate as the soft suggestion of "We need to do something about this" rises to a clamor by the end of an after-school meeting hour. The topics that often arouse the most rage are salary cuts, layoffs, and, of late, defending our profession against the current fetish of politicians and sneaky journalists—standardized test scores, specifically, the push to use those numbers to evaluate educators and ultimately, I suspect, tie our salaries to such flimsy data. Even in kindergarten, where I taught for 10 years, the slow creep of using of multiple-choice tests to measure a 5-year-old's learning and a teacher's teaching has become more and more prevalent. But I want to offer three anecdotes about educating that probably wouldn't even be considered, or rather weren't considered, during the 2010 series of articles by *Los Angeles Times* journalist Jason Song, articles meant to surprise and shame public-school teachers with standardized test scores.

Story I: Esmeralda*

Her name was Esmeralda, like an Andalusian flamenco dancer or a tragic opera protagonist. She looked extremely young for her age. Her enrollment paperwork claimed she'd just arrived from El Salvador and was supposedly 5 years old, but she looked 3 and a half. I realize El Salvador doesn't produce the biggest people in the world, but Esmeralda seemed unusually diminutive and dwarfish. She was terribly cute, with more eyes than face, or hands and legs for that matter. I don't know if she was legally a "little person," but she seemed near the qualification. In fact, I don't even know if she was legal, period. I had a suspicion that her mother needed childcare more than schooling for her youngest daughter, so she was pushing Esmeralda off as a school-aged citizen. But all Esmeralda had to do was giggle and flash her huge dark eyes, and all subterfuge was forgotten. It wasn't my job to police educational opportunities.

Esmeralda hated me from the very second she laid eyes on me. In her toddler eyes, I must've looked like a giant walking nose and mustache, sinister and comic at the same time. Fortunately for her, I was not assigned as her direct kindergarten teacher. Instead, she was assigned to my classroom partner, Jacky, who was beautiful, compassionate, and Guatemalan. Jacky and I shared the room, so Esmeralda wasn't completely rid of the sight of me. I would often catch her stealing glances in my direction, probably trying to figure out how a giant nose and mustache could talk or walk.

Jacky and I soon discovered that Esmeralda was about as ready for kindergarten as a puppy. She exhibited the behavior of laboratory chimpanzees before they learn American Sign Language. She was kind of like a mild Helen Keller but without the excuses; because Esmeralda could see, hear, and talk—or kind of talk. She giggled-screamed more than she spoke. Asking her to draw a circle was like asking her to copy the frescos of the Sistine Chapel. She looked at pencils as if they were magic twigs. Obviously, this little child-puppy-chimpanzee-thing needed a lot of attention, but whenever I approached her she would run away and hide from me as if we were playing tag. She probably thought I, the talking mustache-nose-entity, was trying to inhale her. I left most of the work to Jacky.

What I didn't understand about this whole situation was how Esmeralda's mother didn't ever see what Jacky and I were noticing about Esmeralda's behavior and slow development. Had no one in the household noticed for the supposed five years of Esmeralda's life that she acted like a baby koala? The child couldn't identify colors, didn't know her full name or age, and spoke in a giggle-scream dialect. We would have referred her immediately for testing, but we needed the consent, participation, and advocacy of her mama in order to make the process urgent. We needed her mama to step up and be a concerned parent. When we approached her mother about Esmeralda's issues, we were met with a big "So what?" Then caca day came.

Jacky had her class engaged, writing in their daily journals. Esmeralda, too, sat calmly doing whatever she did in her journal. No one really knew what she did. I was sitting nearby, engaged in some paperwork when I inhaled deeply and then paused. I inhaled again, but this time with kindergarten-teacher olfactory awareness. With the second inhalation I caught it exactly. I stopped my work and looked at Jacky with wide eyes and raised eyebrows. I sniffed loudly. That's kindergarten teacher code for Shit Alert.

We had been partners for so long, Jacky knew exactly what I was asking with my wide-eyed sniffing. Feces patrol had begun. Cruising around separate parts of the classroom, we began taking light, cautious sniffs above the heads of all the suspects. Our noses settled on Esmeralda. Placidly sitting in her seat, she was scribbling out the Gauss Jordan method of finite mathematics.

"Esmeralda, do you have to go to the restroom?" Jacky inquired nonchalantly.

Esmeralda looked up with her black marble eyes and smiled the cutest smile and nodded her head emphatically without a sound. However, with Esmeralda you could never tell whether she understood what was being asked of her. I could have asked her, "Esmeralda, do you like Madonna's latest album?" and she would've given the same happy nod. But this time she seemed to understand. She got up from her seat and moseyed out the door, presumably to the restroom,.

Five minutes passed

Ten.

Fifteen.

Finally, she returned, all smiles.

"Oh, Esmeralda," Jacky sighed. It looked as if Esmeralda had wrestled with a giant, melting chocolate bunny. She had given him a run for his money, but he got in some good licks. Streaks smeared across her chin, on her forearm, and caked in the small of her small back. Where her uniform blouse was half tucked into her underwear were the giant chocolate bunny's remains. She stood there, smiling and as pleased with herself as she could be.

"Esmeralda, what happened?" Jacky asked.

It was a stupid, useless question for so many reasons. We knew what had happened, sort of, and she didn't understand us anyway. Besides, I'm sure, she never really could have explained it to us completely. She stood there, shit-streaked and smiling, as two adults scrambled to and fro, like excited hens, trying to figure out how to take her to the nurse's office to call her mom without actually touching her or getting the audience of kindergarten kids riled up. I was just glad she didn't like to get near me.

We got her escorted to the nurse's office. I don't actually remember who escorted her. Later, we got her assessed and she qualified for special education. Her mom came to the appropriate meetings and signed the appropriate papers. We got Esmeralda what she presumably needed. She had flunked kindergarten, but that was all right because the second time around she was just the right size. The chocolate bunny never assaulted her again.

This is not to suggest that shitting on oneself is a daily occurrence in elementary school, but it is one of a plethora of variables that keep a teaching day in flux; during the school day, there are also the fights and fire drills, and the day of the bike safety assembly, and the day of a student's absence because of a court hearing or asthma, and the week the school's air conditioning fails, the week the teacher is off to mandated training, the week the global pandemic flu visits the school, the month the USC Dental Trailer arrives to offer free mobile dental care, and then the week and a half in May when state testing occurs and the campus falls into a silence, a hopeful silence, that also carries the depressing concern that, under No Child Left Behind legislation, even if we raise our scores we can still be considered failures—again.

Kindergartners, however, don't participate in state testing. During testing time, they are corralled into our cafeteria for recess so that their noisy playing won't disturb the older kids trapped in their classrooms darkening bubbles with number 2 pencils.

My housemate's fourth-grade nephew once commented that he knew of students who, after a certain point of tediousness, just bubble-in random bubbles on the answer sheet so that they can get through it faster. That didn't surprise me. While the *Los Angeles Times* wants teachers held accountable to the tests, students aren't even themselves held accountable to them. Students could play connect-the-dots on their test sheets, and it would have no effect on their report cards or on their promotion to the next grade. Maybe the picture the city's newspaper and Mr. Song offered over the course of 2010 was incredibly incomplete, and maybe what little Esmeralda learned in two years of kindergarten should be measured more in flushes or plies of toilet paper than in darkened bubbles.

Story II: Jose

The fourth grader looked up at me and asked: "Do you remember me? Do you know my name?"

I said, "Of course I do, Jose." And he smiled at me, glad for the affirmation of familiarity as he went off to lunch. I didn't add, "I remember that you shit in your pants when I taught kindergarten intervention."

A kindergartner's instructional attention span is so brief that I try to break up lessons with song and dance every 10 minutes or so. This after-school class I taught for kindergartners who needed extra lessons was no different. I had about 15 kids in my class. Once, I was going over the alphabet when I noticed the children starting to get restless. I decided it was Hokey Pokey time. Yay! We all got up and started putting our right feet in, and our right feet out, shaking them all about, etc., etc., when I noticed that Jose was waaaaay too into the dance. He excitedly bounced around like he was never going to be able to dance the Hokey Pokey again. My teacher instinct kicked in. "What's wrong with you, Jose?" He looked at me as if he didn't know what I was talking about. "Do you have to go to the bathroom?" I surmised.

"Oh yeah," he said as if he had forgotten, and then he flew out the door before I said he could go.

A long, long time passed. I actually forgot he was in the restroom. Almost half an hour later, he returned, walking slowly into the classroom with one hand hidden behind his back and the other lifted with the palm outward like he was gesturing for me to stop. He began announcing, unprompted: "It's alright. It's alright! Mr. Villegas."

I was like: "What's alright? What are you talking about?"

"It's alright. It's ok!" He kept gesturing for me to stop even though I was calmly sitting in my teacher's chair.

I was like, "What's alright?" raising my voice, getting more nervous. I stood up to approach him, realizing that if a child announces out of the blue that everything is alright, something is wrong.

Then he admitted, "I poo-ed in my pants." He brought his hand forth from behind his back. In his hand he held his cartooned underwear, shit stained, all balled up. He might as well have shown me his intestines because I recoiled, immediately going into a gag. OK. OK. OK. What do I do? What do I do? I asked myself. I slowly backed away from him.

"Let me get a bag," I told him. I just happened to have had a Bloomingdale's Big Brown Bag. I use the small, medium and big bags in a lesson I learned from one of my colleagues. I told Jose, "Here's a bag," and I opened it up to hand it to him so he could place his underwear in it himself. I was fighting back the urge to gag aloud again. All of a sudden, in true little-boy style, he turned the opening of the bag into a basketball game. He held his caca underwear as if it were a basketball and he were Michael Jordan at the free-throw line ... no, scratch that, as if he were Shaquille O'Neil at the free-throw line. I screamed, "NOOOOOO!" But nevertheless he shot the dirty underwear at me, trying to make the "basket."

I saw the small, balled-up, shit-stained bundle unfurl in the air as it flew toward me in slow motion. I projected that it would land on my hand. I moved the bag to help his toss sink into it appropriately. In those few seconds, I drew an intense sweat. I closed the bag once the underwear had safely settled at the bottom. I told Jose to go to the office. "They will call your mom," I told him. He cheerfully exited the class, clasping the oversized Bloomingdale's bag in his small hands.

I called the office and gave a heads up to Jesse, the male office secretary. I told him to be discreet. However, when Jose arrived, Jesse asked with a smirk, "Hey little dude, what's in the bag?"

People usually want their names in the paper. That's the whole premise behind cheesy wedding announcements, expensive advertisements, and solemn obituaries. I remember being happily surprised when the *Los Angeles Times* offered a respectful obituary to the New York drag queen Pepper LaBeija; how nice of them. But unless you die, receive an award from some civic club, are selling something, or are about to get married, the only way to be in the paper is to be the "man bites dog" story. Newspapers use their town crier statures to purposely and publicly disgrace the likes of convicted pedophiles or corrupt politicians.

For the *Los Angeles Times* to create its own database and decide for itself who it thinks is effective and not effective in the school district, and to publish the names of those people is arrogant and overstepping. Essentially, Mr. Jason Song and his employers have equated public-school teachers with public figures. They have mistakenly broadened the public portion of the "public school teacher" moniker and merged us with the likes of mayors, judges, and CEOs, despite the fact that we are neither elected nor appointed to our positions. We are hired. We go through both degree and credentialing programs, a battery of state- and district-mandated exams (which we pay for ourselves), unpaid training, mentoring, and evaluation. We are employees who have signed contracts with the school districts, *not with the Los Angeles Times*. If being paid by the government strips us of any confidentiality, then why are police officers and firefighters, public health nurses, corrections officers, and sanitation workers not publicly evaluated and ranked as well?

Why? Because the Los *Angeles Times* and Jason Song believe that the power of public shaming of teachers will somehow improve education. They believe that the proverbial dunce caps placed on teachers' heads will somehow make teaching better. They have used their power and influence to shame without providing any material assistance to schools, teachers, students, or parents and have left behind schools full of demoralized staffs and, in one instance, possibly prompted the suicide of a fifth-grade teacher.

Around the same time in 2010, a Ugandan newspaper, *Rolling Stone*, published the names and addresses of 100 gays and lesbians in their country. Homosexual acts are illegal in Uganda and, as a public service, the periodical decided to expose the "criminals" for their arrest. The model of publishing the identities of private citizens in the name of a public service seems remarkably similar to what the *Los Angeles Times* has decided to do. Obviously, what is considered corrupt or criminal differs from country to country, but the bullying tactics remain the same. I'm sure journalist Jason Song and his employers feel just as much noble pride in their exposé as the Ugandan newspaper.

Story III : Eunice

Her name was Eunice. She was a pretty, blonde, blue-eyed girl who looked more Norwegian than Mexican. Petite. Clean. Hair always brushed. Too cute. Sometimes she could be a little bit of a mean girl, but still always darling. Her mother always did a great job of grooming her. She also adorned her with lots of jewelry. I've noticed Latino parents love to drape their children with precious metals and jewels usually in the shapes of crucifixes. Eunice was a girly girl, wearing shoes with little heels, lip gloss, and bright girl-thingies in her hair. Her jewelry consisted of crosses, virgins and other Catholic regalia. All of it real gold. Not cheap. It was as if she were dipped in a cathedral every day before she went to school.

Once during the mad last 10 minutes of the school day, when my class of 20 kids were retrieving their backpacks and jackets and homework folders and the phone was ringing and someone had forgotten this and another person had forgotten that, Eunice asked if she could go to the restroom. I was like: "Sure. Yeah. Whatever. Go." While I continued to rush around, trying to get everyone and everything in order before the bell rang, I soon realized that Eunice had returned and was standing right beside me like a hungry squirrel. "I dropped my bracelet," she announced.

I wasn't paying much attention, so I said, "Go pick it up."

Eunice instead went to solicit a classmate as a lobbyist. Now there were two squirrels beside me, and the second repeated, "Mr. Villegas, Eunice dropped her bracelet."

Once someone else started soliciting my attention, I realized there was more to this headline than I had first thought. "Where?" I asked.

"In the restroom."

Again the teacher instinct, which had developed more by this year in my career. "Show me," I said.

Eunice escorted me to the restroom. She led me to the toilet, where a big yellow-brown log was floating above a shiny gold bracelet that had sunk to the bottom of the bowl. As far as I was concerned, the bracelet was the lost treasure of El Dorado. That gold bracelet was one flush away from heading into the Pacific Ocean. Sorry, you're asked out, I thought.

But then she looked at me with big, blue expectant eyes, and I thought to myself, OK, Mr. Villegas, come on, you're a problem solver, figure this out. I raced to the classroom sink and retrieved a pair of yellow rubber gloves. I decided we could turn this dilemma into a character-building lesson for Eunice. I approached her with the gloves and told her: "Here. Put on the gloves and get your bracelet yourself."

She shook her head, no.

OK, now I see how it works, I surmised. The light-skinned 5-year-old girl is actually born expecting the dark brown man to reach his hand into a toilet bowl to retrieve her sparkly gold bracelet. Thank God we don't live in 17th-century Mexico, because I'm sure my kindergarten duena would've had me whipped for not following orders. I thought to myself, girlfriend, you're cute and all, but I'm not going there.

Then the school bell rang, and a light bulb went on in my head before flushing. "Eunice, let's wait for your mom," I told her. When her mom arrived, she was the lovely mom I had known since the beginning of the year and she was true to form. Without hesitation or qualm, Eunice's mama slipped on those yellow rubber gloves, dunked her hands into the toilet, retrieved the gold bracelet, and then flushed. At that moment I realized the difference between parents and teachers.

Ultimately, the mama has to do the dirty work, the papa has to do the hard work, the legal, loving guardian is the common denominator during all the changes and personalities a student will encounter from preschool to 12th grade and, hopefully, beyond. But parents don't get publicly evaluated as "most or least effective" by the Los Angeles Times. Nor is parenting evaluated by a standardized test and recorded in some database. Parents also don't get paid or sign contracts to be parents.

We can continue the discussion about how to evaluate teacher effectiveness out of context, but the cheap shot of publicizing the names of teachers on the Internet or in newspaper articles doesn't take into context the complexity involved when, for example, in the middle of learning the alphabet a 5-year-old waits too long to ask to go to the bathroom and starts crying amidst a yellow puddle in front of his classmates. A Los Angeles Times-reading parent might be asked, "How do you want your child treated by that teacher?" Or does what matters most come down to Jason Song tabulating how well the school filled in the bubbles during a week and half in May.

So, I looooooooove to see teachers get riled up because they can turn bad jokes into revolution.

*Names have been changed because, unlike the Los Angeles Times, my intention is not to humiliate people.

gracias.

Christian Bracho

Annette Moore

Sun Cha

Monica Palacios

Terry Wolverton

Allison Engel

Gwin Wheatley

Noe Montes

Hank Henderson

Nikolái Ingistov-García

Richard B. Villegas

Alma D. Villegas

Natalie Villegas

Salvador Villegas

Photo: Noe Montes

Richard Villegas Jr. is a 1974 Ysteléi cabernet aged for three decades in the California oak-lined basin of the mega-pubelo L.A.-titlan. Belvedere Elementary, Our Lady of Lourdes, Bosco Tech, UCLA, and USC were the institutions. T-parties, Tempo, and Tuesdays at a club formerly known as Woody's were the situations .

Villegas loves walks on the beach, Free Cuba! drinks, his Smurf village app, banda (Serbian or Mexican) and purposefully mixing the sacred with the profane. He labors on a novel and works to ultimately free himself of an indentured servitude administered concurrently by LAUSD and, la cabrona, Ms. Salliemae.

www.richardvillegas.com
babybluebabylon@gmail.com

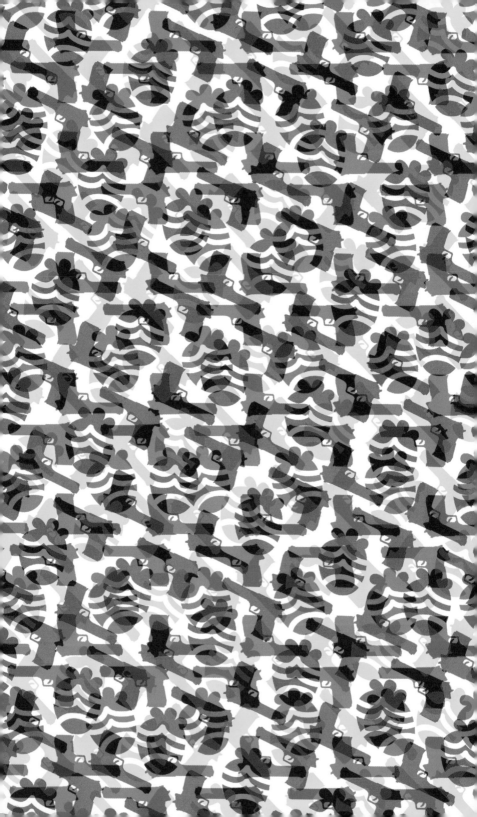

Made in the USA
Charleston, SC
07 August 2016